EAST FROM WEST

by Gabriel Peter

PublishAmerica
Baltimore

© 2007 by Gabriel Peter.
All rights reserved. No part of this book may be reproduced, stored in a retrieval system or transmitted in any form or by any means without the prior written permission of the publishers, except by a reviewer who may quote brief passages in a review to be printed in a newspaper, magazine or journal.

First printing

All characters in this book are fictitious, and any resemblance to real persons, living or dead, is coincidental.

At the specific preference of the author, PublishAmerica allowed this work to remain exactly as the author intended, verbatim, without editorial input.

ISBN: 1-4241-7901-7
PUBLISHED BY PUBLISHAMERICA, LLLP
www.publishamerica.com
Baltimore

Printed in the United States of America

Chapter 1

He vomited himself into consciousness, throwing up across the windshield. He spit and sputtered out what remained in his throat, eyes clasped shut until wiping his face with his hand. There in his palm a mixture of body fluids, none of which he could identify—a colorless glint in what little light shown into the vehicle. He reached out and placed his hands on the steering wheel, tilting his head to the side, but in such weakness his head dropped to dangle again at the end of his neck.

He tried to utter sound, but it only made him gag. His body wretched like he would throw up again, but he managed to control it. Settling his nausea, he winced at the agonizing pain in his left shoulder, supporting the weight of his body in the seatbelt. After a few groanings, his speech evolved into words: "Is everyone alright?" He looked at the passenger seat next to him; there was no one there. No one in the back seat either—the two occupants were lying on the ceiling.

The passenger side of the windshield was broken out. He squirmed in his inverted position to see through the crystallized pattern of broken glass, but it was no use. He was only making himself sick again.

Lights. Then sirens. The last he saw. The last he heard. Before he blacked out again.

"Why did you say that?" the detective asked.

"Hm?" the driver asked from his hospital bed, looking up in a daze.

"Why did you ask if everyone was alright if you couldn't remember who you were with?"

He stared at the baby blue in his blanket, letting color fill his eyes. He swallowed, widened his mouth, feeling his aching jaw click, and said, "I don't know. Immediate reaction I guess."

"But you don't know the names of anyone you were with?"
He shook his head. "No."
"Who did your wife go home with?"
He shifted his eyes again, this time focusing on the doorknob. He was starting to see the whole of the objects he was looking at now. He could see more of the door than he had been able to beyond his direct line of sight.
"Mr. West?" the detective said. "Abel?"
He looked at the detective, and could see his whole face and at least his shoulders. "I'm not married," he said.
"You don't remember being married?" the psychologist asked.
Abel shook his head. "No."
"That woman right there," he pointed. "Can you identify her?"
He looked at her. His eyes trailed over the people around her. Everyone here, in this room—so much pain. "No," he said, and watched the woman when he said it. She didn't flinch.
"How about that man there?" the psychologist asked. "Can you identify him?"
Abel looked at him, long and hard. He squinted at him and wasn't quite sure he was really looking at who he thought he was looking at. In fact, that was impossible. "He looks like my dad," he said.
"How about that man there?" he pointed to another. "Do you know who he is?"
"I want to go home," Abel said.
"How about this person?" the prosecutor asked, sliding a picture in front of him. "Do you know who this is?"
"No, but I've been shown this picture before," Abel said.
Before he could finish what he was saying, the prosecutor had shoved another one at him. "How about this picture? Do you remember who this is?"
"No, I've never…"
"And this person? Who's this? Can you identify this person?"
"Objection, Your Honor," the defense shot up. "He's badgering the witness."

"Overruled," the judge commandeered. "Answer the question."

"Who is this?" the prosecutor demanded.

"I'm telling you, I don't know!"

"These people," the prosecutor howled to the judge and everyone present, "were in the car with this man, this killer, this murderer, while he was driving under the influence of alcohol!"

"Objection, Your Honor. Unsubstantiated evidence. The prosecution is speculating."

"Thank you, Mr. Trask. Sustained. Mr. Rowe, you may…"

"I have no further questions, Your Honor."

"I can testify that the patient is, without a doubt, suffering from a severe case of amnesia. He has no memory of events that transpired in the hours or even years prior to the accident."

"And that is your professional opinion, Doctor?" the defense asked.

"I give no other kind," the doctor half-smiled.

"How many drinks would you say Abel West," the prosecutor pointed at him, "had that night?"

"I'm not exactly for sure," the witness on the stand said. "I saw him with a bottle of Silver, and then he was always refilling his glass of something after that."

"Just one bottle of Silver?"

"Well," she contemplated, "he could have had more than one. But I don't know for sure."

"How many parties have you been to that Abel West was also in attendance?"

"Oh, lots," the witness said.

"By lots," the prosecutor expanded, "you mean, how many? A dozen? Two dozen?"

"More than thirty," the witness said.

"Thank you. And at any one of these parties, have you ever known Abel West not to drink?"

"No," she said. "He always leaves drunk."

"Thank you, Ms. Cordes. No further questions, Your Honor."

The defense was up next. "Ms. Cordes, did you clearly see Mr. West with a bottle of Silver?" he asked.

"Yes, sir. I identified it exactly."

"Did you ever see him open that bottle of Silver? Physically open the bottle and drink it?"

"No. But I mean; it was an open bottle."

"Did you ever see him open any bottle that night?"

"No."

"So you don't know for sure that he had more than one bottle, do you?"

"No. But he was drinking other drinks that night."

"What color were those other drinks?"

"I beg your pardon?"

"You said to the prosecution," he indicated, "that you saw him with an occasionally refilled glass during the evening. What color was the liquid in his glass?"

"He was drinking Silver," she said. "He always drinks that or a rum and Coke. We would tease him for drinking the sissy drinks."

"What color is Silver, Ms. Cordes?"

"Well," she said, "it's clear."

"So it's colorless," the defense said.

"Yes."

"Isn't water also colorless?"

"Yes."

"Would you please state your name and occupation for the court?" the defense lawyer asked.

"Police Officer Mike Murphy of the Lane County Police Deparment."

"Officer Murphy, what is your relation to the incident? What role did you play in all of this?"

"I was the first officer on the scene of the accident."

"How did you know about the accident?"

"We received a call from a witness that had swerved to miss the weaving vehicle," the officer said, "and responded to the report of a single-car accident."

"And what did you find there?"

"We found an overturned Cadillac Escalade lying on its top in the ditch on the opposite side of the road facing into oncoming traffic. We estimated that it had rolled four and a half times before it got there. About twenty feet out in front of the vehicle in the oncoming lane of traffic was the body of twenty-four year old Darrel Druse. In the vehicle were the remaining two passengers, Frank Meadows and David Solis, and the driver, Abel West."

"From your investigation, what did you determine had happened?"

"From what we can tell," the officer said, "it was an issue of miscalculating the curve. Witness accounts stated that the Escalade was swerving and not staying in its own lane. Coming around the turn on that side of the hill, it was almost entirely in the opposite lane. The driver had been startled by the oncoming headlights, and turning the wheel at his speed caused the vehicle to roll."

"So whoever was driving the Escalade," the defense said, "was still aware enough to respond to other traffic."

"I suppose so."

"Were there witness accounts from anyone else other than from those in the oncoming car?" the defender asked.

"No, there were not," the officer said.

"So how do you suppose the people in that car would have been able to see that the Escalade was swerving prior to it coming around that side of the hill?"

The prosecution rose to object. "Speculative answer, your honor."

"Sustained," the judge said. "Please move on, Mr. Trask."

"Sorry, your honor," the defense lawyer said, and went back to the officer. "What was the state of the passengers when you arrived?"

"Darrel Druse was dead on arrival. The three persons still in the vehicle were still alive. David Solis died that morning at the hospital, and Frank Meadows remains in a coma."

"What of Abel West?"

"Well," the officer pointed, "he's sitting over there at that table."

"I mean, what were his vital signs?"

"Oh, he was unconscious. He regained consciousness en route to the hospital."

"Did you have Abel West's blood-alcohol level tested after the accident, Officer Murphy?"

"No, sir. We didn't."

"Did the hospital give you any records or show you any indication that Mr. West had been driving under the influence?"

"No, they didn't. But they didn't give us confirmation of any kind."

"Is it not customary at the scene of an accident to ask the level of toxicity in a person's blood?"

"Not necessarily at the accident, but from the hospital records we are able to decipher…"

"So why don't you know Mr. West's from that night?"

"We were trying to save as many passengers as we could regardless of the circumstance. We were just worried about keeping those alive who were still alive."

"Officer Murphy, did anyone in the vehicle, as best as you can tell, have their seatbelts fastened?"

"Only one," said the police officer.

"Which occupant was that?"

"The driver, Abel West."

"Officer Murphy, how long have you been on the force?"

"I've been on the force for almost twenty years."

"How many drunk-driving fatalities have you handled in those twenty years? And I'm just talking about the fatalities."

"I'm not sure," officer Murphy pondered. "I would say more than twenty."

"In how many of those accidents," the defense said, "can you honestly recall the drunk driver was wearing his seatbelt?"

"Only once," the officer said.

"And when was that?"

"That was Abel West."

The defender chuckled. "But you just said that you don't have medical proof that Abel West was intoxicated, didn't you?"

The officer didn't say anything.

"So in reality, you've never encountered a drunk-driving accident in which the drunk driver was wearing their seatbelt, have you?"

"I guess not."

"No further questions, Your Honor."

The steps in front of the court house were crowded with press, media, fans, protestors, rushing toward the exhausted defense once they emerged from the building. Microphones were shoved into Abel's face, in front of the lawyer, and dangling over the head of the blonde that stepped in between them, taking hold of Abel's hand. Feeling her fingers lace into his, Abel looked at her in surprise, her eyes focused downward, watching the steps as they were ushered forward. A barrage of questions and assertions fired around them, no single voice above the rest, all muddled in the sound of the mob. The three were led through the mass by security, police, and other miscellaneous crew, dividing the throng for passage. They stepped into the limo parked on the street curb, door open, and as soon as they were inside closing safely around them.

The driver escaped the swarm of people. Abel's breath had quickened. He hadn't noticed until all was still and silent again. When he realized he was making his tense state evident to other passengers, he took a fistful of his shirt at his chest, relaxing himself. He looked at the woman next to him, his lawyer across from him. The lawyer looked back with a gaze that was different now—not like the caring, abiding counsel that he had been. It was the look of a stranger. Or rather: the look of someone that saw Abel as a stranger; cold and unaccepting. The business was over. The lawyer had done his job. They were now back to names in each other's rolodex.

All stares, glances, gestures extended to him over the past few months seemed so pitiful. Not one of them familiar. Even after being freed by the court's decision, rescued from the pit of blame, Abel still felt he was drowning in a sea of contempt. No one had to say a word. The lack of empathy held his head beneath the surface.

He turned to his wife, the woman sitting next to him. She was looking out her window. He was still holding her hand. He hadn't noticed. "Sorry," he said, for no reason other than wanting to communicate something to someone—in whatever way he could.

He retreated to the window on his side where he remained until the first stop of the ride.

"This is mine, Manny," the lawyer indicated, tapping on the glass behind him. Taking up his briefcase and coat, he said to Abel, "Your wife has agreed to take you home. Some of the families of the deceased are going to follow-up with their own lawsuits. We'll handle it. I'll call you if I need anything."

The door opened for him and he placed one foot out on the street, stopping when Abel said his name: "Trask." He turned back. "Thanks," Abel said. "Really. For everything."

The lawyer only nodded before stepping out. Not to their surprise, the press was waiting at the office. As the car pulled away, Abel's eyes followed the lawyer until he was looking out the back window at the gathering on the sidewalk, almost sad to see him go. This lawyer, Trask, was the only constant in his life in recent days.

After a spell, he turned back to face forward and sighed. Abel felt friendless again, even in the presence of what should be familiar company. He wanted to talk to her so badly. "Thank you," would be a good start: for sitting through the court proceedings, for taking him home. He wished she'd be the first to speak. He had no idea how to communicate with this woman. He didn't know what to say. It was probably best. Yes, saying anything would just create more tension at this point. Still, Abel kept a hand on the seat, just in case she might notice his hand close by enough to hold again.

He rest his head against the window, watching the tops of trees pass by as they drove. The sky seemed gray and heavy, appearing even darker through the tinted windows. The neighborhoods had changed, but they weren't yet out of the city—not entirely. He felt tired, but didn't want to sleep, afraid of what else might change when he woke up again.

When the car slowed and began to turn, Abel brought himself to pay more attention to the scene they were in. They came to a stop, then upon moving forward again passed a booth with a raised crossing gate.

The vehicle slowly progressed into a protected neighborhood. Every house was luxurious, separated from the next by either a generous amount of space or a high wall. Some were very open and others well-covered beneath a canopy of trees. An occasional few were completely secluded behind walls on all sides, but the driveway they pulled into led to a house with an open yard, seen beautifully from the street. The landscape was meticulously designed in its placement of trees, bushes, stones and pathways.

The driver opened the door on the wife's side and Abel waited a second or two before he followed after her. When he walked into the house, she had placed her carried items on the couch and stood there with her back to him. He quietly shut the door and put his hands in his pockets, looking around at the spacious enclosure. He thought he might have been able to recognize his home. He did not. For the first time in months, now outside of hotel rooms and courthouses, surrounded by people and places that should be familiar, he wondered exactly how much of his memory he had lost.

"I suppose I should be the first to say something," said his wife.

Abel was relieved at her willingness to speak to him, getting over the barricade that separated them. "Rebecca, I just want to tell you…"

She promptly put up another wall. "Abel, don't apologize to me again. Please."

He licked his lips, feeling extremely dry. "I don't know what to say."

Rebecca turned herself toward him and crossed her arms, still several paces between them. She didn't appear angry. Or sympathetic. It was a flat canvas she presented; dull of color or expression. Even so, she was a beautiful creature, blonde hair pulled back, accentuating her slender neck and smooth features. Very little make-up made her natural beauty evident. Her small shoulders raised and lowered with a deep and silent breath.

"How long have we lived here?" Abel asked.

"Three years."

"Where did we live before here?"

"In a penthouse. I didn't like it there," she added. "Neither did you. But you never admitted that."

"What do you do?" he asked.

"What do I do?"

"Yeah," he said. "Are you just…my wife? Do you have a career? Do you do something?"

She stared at him for a good while before she answered his question. "I work for a publishing company. I've been trying to start my own firm."

"How's that coming?"

"Slow."

Abel nodded and moved from where he stood, still looking around, mostly at the ceiling and high corners. "And we don't have any children," he said.

She closed the distance between them, marching toward him rather quickly. Her approach was sudden and startling enough it almost made Abel take a step back away from her. He thought she was going to hit him.

"Tell me you don't remember anything," she said, raising her voice, pointing her finger at him. "Tell me this wasn't all just a ruse; some ploy to keep you out of a nasty jail sentence from driving under the influence. I know how much you drink at those parties. I don't care if you don't want to fess up for your mistakes, Abel. I've rather come to expect this kind of behavior from you. Just don't look at me as though you don't know me or you don't owe me anything. I will not be a part of this."

He bit his lip, truly attempting to find some reassurance for her, but he couldn't. She had already denied him any sort of apologia. There was nothing.

A loud obtruding knock came at the door and Rebecca retreated from sight leaving Abel to care for this foreign house on his own. He went to the door and opened up to an unusual and unexpected welcome: a person of resplendent enthusiasm.

"Abel! Buddy! What's happening?" This peacock-ish individual slapped Abel on the chest and walked right in, making the air his bullhorn: "Who do I have to sleep with to get a scotch in this place?" He turned back to Abel. "I'm sorry. You probably gave the staff the week off or something. Give yourself some space. Time to recoup. That's fine. That's good. Hey, just so you know, I've been canceling appointments left and right, but you've got one this weekend—a writing session for an upcoming movie. Said they wanted you."

Abel wasn't processing any of this. "I'm sorry," he said, "my wife and I were just…"

"She'll come around. Don't worry about it. She always has. You have a very forgiving wife. You'd have to in order to be you and stay married for six years."

"I was told five years," Abel said.

"Your anniversary was during your trial, genius. Her favorite flower is the tulip. Remember that."

Abel stood there rather dumbfounded.

"I'm sorry. Where's my head at?" the visitor said. "I'm Felson MacGreggor. I'm your agent-slash-manager-slash-errand-boy-slash-fall-guy and whatever else is in the job description. I signed exclusively with you about half a year ago before the whole, well, thing. I hate the name Felson, so everyone calls me Greg. In fact, you're the only one in this business that knows my first name is Felson, and we've always kept that between us. I could have just skipped the whole 'Felson' part altogether, and then you never would have known, would you?"

Abel still looked a little confused. The agent walked up close to him and said softly; "So, now that I've revealed my secret, let's hear yours. Are you really," he knocked himself on the head and then made a motion like a bird was flying by, "or is this all just an act? You can trust me, here. This stuff stays between us."

"Um, Greg," Abel started, "listen, my wife and I have had quite a week with all this litigation stuff. Is it a problem that we can't do this some other time?"

"Come on," the agent said. "Just a sampling. Just a little. Hey, you might be in here bed-ridden, waited on hand and foot and all of that, but while you're taking it easy, I'm the one covering for you talking to all these reporters. I'm the one taking the heat out there for you. I gotta at least look like I know what I'm talking about."

Abel sighed; a bit of exasperation mixed in with his sorrow. "I don't remember anything, Greg. For at least a good dozen years. Maybe more."

"Good." The agent stuck out his hand. "My name is actually Tom Gregory. I'm a reporter with the *Los Angeles Sun Times*. I was just testing you."

Abel cocked his head. "I beg your pardon?"

"I'm just jerking your chain man." He smacked Abel on the chest again. "Have you ever heard of the *Los Angeles Sun Times*? But you do have to be careful with who you talk to. People will be testing you, and you have no idea whether you can or can't remember anyone."

"So wait," Abel said, "is your name Felson or Todd?"

"That's Tom," the agent said. "And the answer is neither. My name is actually Al Cohol. Stay away from me: I'll mess you up."

Abel wasn't amused.

"I'm sorry," the agent laughed. "I shouldn't be having so much fun at your expense. It's Tom Gregory. I am your agent. I wasn't kidding about that part. Honestly. What parent in their right mind would name their kid Felson? But I don't like Tom any more than I like Felson, so you can still call me Greg. Listen, I'll leave you alone for a couple days and get in touch with you before you meet with that writer's group on Saturday to fill you in on all the details. Oh, before I forget, I got you a new cell phone. Here you go. The number comes up when you turn it on. But be careful who you give the number to."

Abel looked at it as strangely as he'd examined everything else the past few months. "Hey, how do I get a hold of you?"

"I'm the only number programmed in there so far," Greg said. "But don't try to call me. I'll call you." He pointed his finger at him like a gun and winked. "Wow, did that sound as corny to you as it did to me? Alright, I'll chat with you latta."

After he was gone, Abel was still looking at the device in his hand and whispered to himself, "Cell phone." What a strange man that was. Abel didn't know what to think of him. Or what to think of anything. He was alone again, in the presence of no one other than himself— to even whom he felt like a stranger. He put his hands in his pockets and walked with small silent steps, watching his feet as though he even needed to re-learn how to walk.

In front of the large fireplace in the living room Abel stood, examining the mantle full of gold statues, so abundant that it extended to shelves on either side. There were awards of every kind; some prestigious honors he recognized by name only and others he hadn't heard of before. All of them paid homage to Abel West. Abel. West. He looked at his name in the polished yellow plate of one of these trophies. The name he recognized. The eyes in its reflection he did not.

In another part of the house, a woman was looking at her own reflection. Rebecca gazed beyond the hazy image of her eyes in the window and out across the yard. It started to rain again. The drops left trails down the panes of glass, tracing the tears that trickled down her cheeks.

Chapter 2

Trial was over. Abel West was declared innocent. But the work was not yet over. Alexander Trask was still issuing statements for the press. With a new development against his client now leaked to news reporters, it was difficult to get any work done without also having to entertain news reporters. Nonetheless, his client's estate paid him well. He was Abel's representative to the end.

Trask stood on the sidewalk in front of his law firm after another long day completing the routine by answering a few questions. "What about this new lawsuit from Darrel Druse's parents?" came the reporters' blurts, in some word fashion all asking the same thing. It would be the only question he'd allow today.

"With every trial," Trask explained, "there are always those that wish to take advantage of an unfortunate situation. I ask you please to be respectful of the families with their grief and other difficulties. Abel West wishes Darrel Druse's parents his condolences and sympathizes with their loss. His family has struggled with loss in the past and have their own obstacles to overcome at the present time. We are going to look into the matter carefully, and to be fair are willing to offer the Druse family a settlement. We hope that they will consider the amount adequate as there's a good chance this case will never see a court room."

More questions shot at the attorney, but Trask ignored them and continued; "There is no indication that the Solis family wants to sue Able West, but he's offering them the same settlement out of compassion. Frank Meadows' medical bills will be paid. I assure you this is all in Abel's good will. Again, please remember that these families are going through difficult times. We are handling all of this the best we can. Accidents happen. Abel West has been cleared of all charges. We need to be able to look past this and move on. Thank you."

Abel walked into the luxurious hotel lobby to be greeted by a shorter balding man, sharply dressed and reaching for Abel's hand. "Hello, Mr. West. I'm Gary Bellows. We appreciate that you're still so willing to work with us despite the circumstances. The writers were insistent they only wanted to work with you. Scheduling is ludicrous for both of us, I'm sure, so we appreciate your consideration. But, hey, I don't want to waste your time. Let's head upstairs."

Bellows had ushered him over to the elevator and pushed the button for the floor. "I'm sorry," Abel said, "do we know one another?"

The agent looked at him with a rather peculiar cockeyed glance. "No," he said. "We've never met before. I talked to your agent. We arranged this meeting of writers to put a song together for an upcoming movie. You got the tidbits on the story already. You're just working on the one song. We haven't landed a singer yet, but Christina is a possibility."

"Who?"

The agent chuckled. "Very funny. But that's a good point. We'd like to go with someone more classical for the type of film we're putting together, but we haven't been able to barter any sort of deal with anyone."

The elevator doors opened. "We've got you a suite down here," Bellows said. "The other writers have already been working for the past hour. Coffee will always be hot, and the bar is open with anything you need." He put his key in the door to the room and pushed it open. "Good morning, fellas," the agent said.

No one said anything. The deemed "writers" all held cigarettes and various alcoholic beverages to their liking. Hotel staff was immediately ready to service Abel, taking his jacket and waiting on him. "Can I get you anything from the bar, sir?"

"No thanks," Abel said. "I don't drink."

Which garnered a few chuckles in the room.

"Cigarette, sir?" he was asked, but merely refused with a hand gesture thinking he'd get another snide reaction if he confessed he didn't smoke.

The agent took Abel by the arm. "Tony Waters you know. The two of you have written together before. This is Billy Matthews, Kirk…"

Tony interrupted. "We've all met, Bellows. Can you get out of here and let us do our job while the nicotine and alcohol are doing theirs?"

"Certainly," he said. "I'll be back up to check in on you fellas in an hour."

"So anyway," Tony started up again, "I think that kind of pattern in the chorus is just too repetitious. It's unnecessary. I think the general theme is spoken without having to say 'The things I' whatever every single time."

"I think it really works," Kirk defended. "I think it needs to stay. It's just these words 'crave' and 'say' don't really work. I mean, do we need to say 'crave'? It even escapes the poetry that's being developed here."

Abel seemed lost without a place to sit, secretly wishing he wasn't there. "Abel, your seat is over here," Tony said. He took his foot off the piano bench and waved him in that direction. "Yeah, okay, so 'say' and 'way' rhyme with one another. Do you want to change 'crave' to another 'ay' word? Then you're rhyming everything."

"No, you wouldn't be, because the rhyme changes in the second half of the chorus."

"Come over here, Abel," Tony said. "This is what we have so far." He set the score with the lyrics down on the piano. "Play a little bit for us and tell us what you think."

Abel rubbed out another pain in his shoulder. "Why don't you play it and I'll listen?"

Tony chuckled. "Because I don't play. I've got that thing in my left hand. Come on. Have a seat."

Abel sat down and looked at the notes on the paper in front of him, the Morse coded combination of black and white dotting and dashing up and down the lines wafting across the page. Placing the four fingers of his right hand upon the ivory polish on the keyboard, looking like he were about to type a letter, he tapped the surface of the piano keys and rubbed back and forth feeling the gap between them, but not applying any pressure.

The group gathered around him, peering over his shoulder and around the sides of the piano waiting eagerly to hear the melody ready to erupt from Abel's creativity. With his index and middle fingers, he picked out two notes and pressed them—a single harmony. Then he picked out three notes and played them, which sounded neither melodic nor from the same key of the previous pair.

Abel snickered, not because he was humored but in absolute estrangement. Still, he tried to summon an ability he was apparently known for. It must be there somewhere. Placing his left hand along the lower pitched keys, he pressed down, playing another triad with his right. Nothing sounded right. Though he didn't know what he was doing, he knew what he was trying to do was wrong.

"Go on, Abel," said Tony. "What have you got?"

Abel placed his hands on the cover of the piano, tapping his thumb for a moment, and finally closed the lid over the keys, shaking his head. "I can't."

"Why not?" asked another.

"Because," Abel said, "I've never played the piano before."

Abel West was one of the industry's most premier songwriters. Having contributed to a hundred artists in many styles and genres, Abel had garnered more than twenty number one songs in the past decade appearing on most every chart with nearly two hundred radio singles to his credit. Some would probably consider Abel the most accomplished songwriter of his time, and certainly one of the most recognized names in liner notes. Record label professionals were familiar with Abel's Midas touch, but the piano player was selective with the projects he took on and quite particular about the writers and artists he worked with. Still, looking for connections or that chance at his next number-one-single was not something he had to chase after anymore. Success and opportunity came to him.

Five years after graduating high school, Abel landed his first number one mainstream single, a 90's pop song called *Be With Me Always,* that made its home quickly at the top of the charts. Before that, he had been the principle songwriter for a rock group called Unto the Breach that never could quite establish their sound. Abel had always been a behind-the-scenes man mostly. There wasn't much limelight popularity in being everyone else's pen and paper. Though most probably wouldn't recognize him if they passed him on the street, his name still held a respect of wealth and talent. He had never gotten as much press in ten years as he was getting now with the headline attention of his car accident.

Darrel Druse was a twenty-four year old R&B overnight pop sensation with help from several tracks written by Abel West, including the current radio hit. Abel had a bit of a hand in producing Darrel's debut project, for which they threw an album release party at a label executive's house upstate. It was at this party, and most others like it, that Abel and his companions got drunk and decided to take a drive. This time, the result of the party ride would kill two passengers including the young rising star, never to know the heights success could take him.

Abel's surviving side-effect was his amnesia, the depth or severity of which was uncertain. To get a better handle on Abel's condition, his wife Rebecca and older brother Jared recruited the help of family psychologist Ellis Corin, who also testified on Abel's behalf in court. The Wests came into Dr. Corin's services after Abel was suspected of having an affair a year ago, which he promptly denied. In order to eschew a costly divorce, Abel agreed to couples counseling under the psychologist of Rebecca's choice. The result didn't have the affect that she had hoped it would.

Their marriage was in shambles and not far from certain demise. However, this accident had brought Rebecca's responsibility in the partnership to the forefront, something she didn't consider herself emotionally capable of handling. Dr. Corin tried to give the two caring family members some assurance.

"We're here," he said to Jeremy and Rebecca, "because of our love for Abel West and a desire to see him come out for the better. In my years of practice, I've never seen a case like this. Most psychologists can go through their entire careers and not witness a patient with amnesia of any kind. I assure you both, it is quite real. Abel has no recollection of the accident or the events leading up to it."

"For how far?" Jared asked. "I was talking with him yesterday and he didn't remember any of his nieces or nephews."

"But he knows who you are," the doctor said. "He doesn't know who Rebecca is. Right now, it's hard to tell. It's difficult to say if his amnesia is selective or if it starts at an actual point in his childhood or young adult life. Do either of you get any indication of childish behavior? Something that would indicate his mind might actually be at a point more in his formative years?"

They both shook their head. "Although," Jared recalled, "He was singing a song the other day when he came over and was visiting with the family. I took him back to my study and showed him some old family albums, hoping that would trigger something in his memory. You told me to ask him lots of questions, so when I heard the tune, I asked him about it."

"What is that you're singing?" Jared asked.
"What?" Abel replied, looking up from his page-turning.
"Just now, you were singing a song."
"Oh, was I? I believe it was 'Where Would I Be' by Harvest. Do you remember that one?"

Jared's face froze as though he were trying to recall the song. He snickered. "Wow. It's been years since I've heard Harvest. I forgot there was even such a group as Harvest."

"Really?" Abel asked. "Good group." And he went back to examining photographs.

"How is that significant?" Corin asked.

"My parents," Jared said, "never let us listen to anything other than Christian music when we were young. That was the rule in the house. Harvest was Abel's favorite group. He started listening to some heavier stuff when he got to college. Or I guess it was after he dropped out. I'm not sure. Honestly, I don't know much about Abel after mom and dad got divorced. I went to live with dad and Abel and my sister lived with mom. I do know that I haven't heard him relate to anything remotely Christian in years."

"Did you ask him about the song?" Corin asked.

"No, I didn't. Should I have?"

"If a memory like that comes up again, ask him how he remembers it. It would be interesting to know if it was flipping through picture albums that made him remember that or it really is one of the fresher memories in his mind."

Rebecca had been pondering over Jared's story of his brother's memories. "You know, I had something similar happen to me."

Rebecca walked into the kitchen, feeling a bit flustered and hurried as mornings later in the week would tend to do to her. She went to the fridge and fetched up her strawberries and blueberries, taking them over to the blender, though the blender was already occupied with its own assortment of fruit. She looked at Abel who was sitting at the table in the middle of the kitchen, reading. "What is this?" she asked.

He looked up. "Oh, it's your breakfast." And lowered his eyes back to his text.

Rebecca was pointedly suspicious. "How did you know I liked this blend for breakfast?"

"Because you've been making it the past three mornings," Abel said. "I noticed you were particularly hurried today, so I put it all in the blender for you."

She watched him for a moment before catching a glance at what he was reading. "What is that? What are you reading?"

"Your Bible," he said.

"Why?" she asked.

"I'm sorry," he said, "it was the only one I could find." Rebecca stared at him long enough to make Abel feel guilty for taking her Bible without permission. "Do you want it back? I won't take it again."

"What made you want to take my Bible?" she asked.

He shrugged. "Because I had nowhere else to turn."

"Oh wow," Jared uttered.

"What did you do after that?" Corin asked.

Rebecca sighed, "I made my breakfast and left."

"You didn't talk to him about it?"

"I didn't know how to," she said. "I mean, conversation has not been his most quality trait over the past couple of years. Or ever. I don't know how I'm supposed to immediately transform just because he has."

"It's obvious that he feels isolated," Dr. Corin said. "But it's not that he's on the outside looking in. He's right in the middle of it. He's been handed this life that he doesn't know. He doesn't recognize. And he is the pinnacle figure of all of it—a person regarded with success and achievement but who lacked the compassion to create comfort among the people around him."

"Doctor," Rebecca said, "you're referring to him as someone completely different. He's still Abel West. He's still my husband. He's the same man I introduced you to."

"Rebecca, he doesn't know who you are," Corin said. "We must entertain the possibility that he may never remember who you are. He has complete and utter memory loss. The Abel West you know is dead. He died in that car accident. The Abel West we have now is a completely different person. We should approach the situation that way. He is also still a member of this family. You must love him like one."

What can I do
To get together with you
When I can't even
Keep my head beneath the clouds
What can I say
That would get your to stay
When I can't even
Keep my feet here on the ground
When getting you is all I think about

"Can we change the station please?" Abel asked.
"Why?" Greg chuckled. "What's wrong with this station?"
"I just don't want to listen to the radio right now."
"Why not? This is your song, you know."
Abel turned the knob off.
"Fine, be that way," Greg smirked. "Like it or not, it's what pays the bills."
"Not today it didn't."
Greg laughed. "How could you just forget how to play the piano? I don't get it! How do you just forget something like that?"
"I apparently didn't start writing songs until I got to college. Did that ever cross your mind?" Abel was even less comfortable with his present company than he was in a hotel suite full of strangers. This man who a few days before had obnoxiously introduced himself at Abel's home, his professed "agent" that he was supposed to call Greg, was ushering him around trying to rehabilitate Abel with his life.

"Hey, man, all this stuff's going to get taken care of," Greg said. "I'm sorry you had a bad writing session today. It happens to the best of us. All this legal stuff will handle itself. You've got absolutely nothing to worry about."

"I don't even know enough to know what it is I'm supposed to worry about."

Greg laughed. "I don't think you quite understand how loaded you are. Do you know how the whole royalty business works?" Abel didn't say anything and tried to feign disinterest. "You basically get a nickel every time a song gets played on the radio," Greg said. "Actually, it's more than that, but the record company needs a little somethin'-somethin' as well as the publisher and other writers if you co-wrote with someone. That song that played right there—money in the bank. And you gotta think: if a hundred stations were playing that song all at the same time, cha-ching, that's money for you. The way that top forty radio works these days, your latest song is playing probably once every ninety minutes on more than two thousand radio stations in North America. Now that Darrel Druse has passed away, everyone's playing that song even more in his memory. The money you're paying the Druse family—Darrel is making it for you."

"Sounds dishonest," Abel said.

"Dishonest?" Greg snickered. "What's dishonest about it? It's your money. You wrote the song. So the situation is unfortunate. So what?"

"So I capitalize on someone else's misfortune? Doesn't sound very honest to me."

"Listen to yourself," Greg said. "Listen to all this philosophical talk. This isn't the Abel I remember."

"Yeah, well it's not the Abel I remember either, Greg."

"I'm going to cancel all of your appointments," Greg said. "You take some time off. Learn the piano a little bit. Wine and dine your wife. Do what you need to do. You'll get your groove back. Hey, how about something to drink—take the edge off?"

"I'll be in the car," Jared said, pulling the door closed behind him as he left the office.

"Something else I can help you with?" Corin asked Rebecca.

She looked up at him for a second with a half smile, lowering her eyes to the floor again. "I wanted to know," she said softly, "if Abel has said anything to you. About me. Or anything. What have you talked about?"

"You know I can't answer that," Corin said. "I understand that you're his wife and he has amnesia but Abel is not helpless. I still have to respect the doctor/patient relationship between us."

She only nodded.

"Maybe if his behavior was more childlike," Corin continued, "I might be able to disclose something to you. But you and Jared already acknowledged that he seems rather mature."

"He is," she said, "probably more mature than he was before the accident."

"The best thing we can do for him now is be his friends. Pray for him. And pray for wisdom that you'll do what's best for both of you and say the right things."

She nodded again, her forehead wrinkling, her face becoming flush. She was wrenching the straps of her pocketbook in her hands. And she began to cry.

"Rebecca, have a seat," Corin said, placing his hand on her arm to escort her to a chair, but she refused. "What's the problem?"

"I wanted so much for him to change," she said, unable to look up from her sobbing. "I prayed for him to change. I wanted our marriage to be alright. I wanted to start all over again. I didn't want it to turn out like this. I didn't mean for this to happen to him."

"Rebecca, this is not your fault," Corin assured. "You did not do this. Abel was the one that put those drinks in Abel's hands. He got behind the wheel of that car. This is his mistake. Not yours. You did not bring this upon him. If anything, you should consider that your prayers protected him. Perhaps it's your prayer that is giving him—you, the both of you—this second chance."

She nodded and stuttered her breath as she tried to collect herself.

"Look at me," Corin said. She lifted her face but her eyes went to the window, or somewhere other than he. "You love him, don't you?"

"Yes. I'm trying."

"Then do exactly that," Corin said. "Just love him. I can say that he's not expecting anything from you. Even what you feel like you can give would be the world to him."

"Thank you, Ellis."

"Hey," he smiled, "it's my pleasure. Come on. Let's pray before you go."

Trask pinched the bridge of his nose and handed his briefcase and overcoat to the house maid. Faithfully, she was there with ibuprofen and a glass of water. She offered to take the glass from him after he had swallowed, but he wanted to keep it with him this time. He walked into the living room where his wife was sitting, reading by lamplight.

He sat on the couch opposite her, resting his glass on the arm next to him, still holding it in hand. She acknowledged his presence with a glance and a half-smile. "Hello," he said. "What have you been doing today?"

"Reading," she said.

"Did you go to work today?" he asked.

"This is work," she indicated.

"I know, but I mean actually getting out of the house."

"No. How are you feeling?"

Trask knew she was just trying to change the subject, but he humored her. "Tired and overworked."

She only smiled, never actually making eye-contact with him.

"I'll be on the news again tonight," he added.

"I'm sorry. I know you hate being on the news. But the publicity is nice."

"I suppose." He took another hardy drink of his water.

"Thank you for keeping me out of all of this," she said. "I don't know that I've formally thanked you for that. Really."

"No thanks are necessary," he said. "If they had put you on the stand, I wouldn't have been able to represent Abel."

"I know. But I appreciate it anyway."

He nodded and reached to quench himself again.

"And I'm sorry."

"I know you are," he said.

She looked toward him longingly this time.

"I wish you would stop saying that. I know you're sorry. If you keep saying that, it detracts from it. It sounds like you're not really sorry."

"I'm sorry. I mean..." She stammered. "I didn't mean that, I just..."

"I know what you meant," he said. "Don't worry about it. I forgive you. That's it. I wish you would move on. I want you to get out of the house again. You need to go back to work."

"I can't go back to work," she said. "It's so hard."

"You don't think it's hard for me?" he replied, raising his voice somewhat. "I have to represent him, for crying out loud. I'm going to be dealing with this matter for the rest of the year."

"I know, but at least he doesn't remember."

"That just makes it easy on him. This is not easy for me."

"See, you're still mad at me."

Trask sighed his frustration. "I am not still mad at you. I have a headache, that's all. And you won't let this go."

"I'm sorry." She put her hand over her mouth with an apprehensive squeak once the words left her mouth. Trask shook his head and got up from his seat. "Where are you going?" she asked him.

"To my study," he said. "And then probably to bed."

"Okay," she said. "Do you want me to leave you alone?"

He stopped with his back still to her. "I can sleep in the bedroom off of the office. I just need to worry about sleeping right now. I'm exhausted."

"Okay."

He turned around and looked at his wife. "It's nothing against you. I promise."

She nodded.

Abel couldn't find comfort in the smoke-hazed bar. The sordid atmosphere weighed heavy on him. Even the sounds around them, though not particularly offensive or tacky, were polluting his senses. The establishment was otherwise upper-scale, a classy kind of joint, but Abel didn't feel relaxed here. It was like he had just walked into the wrong bathroom. Of course, that was something he had been feeling for a while now.

Greg continued talking away about anything and everything Abel West. Abel was beginning to think he was obsessed.

"You had thirty songs on the radio last year, which was the most I think anyone's ever done in a year. Not even Dianne Warren has done that I don't think. They were all in the top twenty in their categories. You probably could have done that again this year, but you started investing time in that Druse kid. Probably wouldn't have been a bad investment if the dumb kid had been wearing his seatbelt. Oh well—you own like his whole album anyway."

"I have a question for you," Abel said.

"Okay," Greg said, taking a swig of his drink. "Shoot."

"If a person owns something, but they don't have any responsibility to it or obligation to it—it doesn't need to be maintained, there's no upkeep involved, it's just yours. But then they forget about it. That it even exists or that it was ever in their possession. Do they still own it?"

Greg nodded and folded his hands, elbows on the bar top, murmuring the occasional "Hm" as he pondered the question. "Okay," he finally said, "I have a question for you."

"Okay."

"If a tree falls in the forest, and no one hears it, is this still a stupid question?"

"What?"

Greg laughed. "What the hell does that mean? Do they still own it? Do they still own what? What are you talking about? If I buy a car, I gotta pay taxes on the stupid thing. I can't just forget about it. The IRS is going to come after me one way or the other. I can't convince them that I just forgot I bought a car."

"I'm not talking about things that you have a responsibility for," Abel said.

"Then what do you mean? Why is this important?"

"Are we in possession of anything?" Abel asked. "Do we ever own anything in the first place? I mean, Frank Meadows is in a coma. He doesn't even have possession of his own consciousness at the moment. When I die, those songs that I own, all of this crap that I woke up from a car accident and suddenly have in my possession—if I had died in that car wreck, all this stuff would go to somebody else. If that's the case, it was never mine in the first place, was it?"

"You are tripping me out," Greg said. "I've heard coke addicts make more sense than you."

"Are we friends?"

"What?"

"Are you and I friends?" Abel repeated. "Did we hang out and we were buddies before? Do you look after me?"

Greg shrugged. "Sure, I guess."

Abel held up the amber liquid in the glass he had not been drinking from. "Then why did you buy me this?"

Greg didn't say anything.

"Take me home, please."

Chapter 3

It had been a long time since Rebecca looked forward to coming home, and tonight was no exception. She secretly hoped that Abel had already gone to bed, but the hint of light in some of the windows suggested where his location was in the house. She sat on her side of the car, silent, looking at her obligatory return.

"Do you want me to come in with you?" Jared asked her.

"I have to be alone with him sometime," she answered, still looking at the house.

"If you need me to take him again," he said, "for the day or whatever, just let me know."

"I'm sure I can handle him." A couple seconds later, she was laughing. "We're speaking about him as though he were a child."

Jared chuckled. "Call me if you need anything."

"I will," she said. "And Jared? Thank you. Really. For everything."

"Anytime," he smiled.

"Tell Emily I said hello."

"Will do."

As much as she didn't feel like being here, Rebecca always loved the smell of her home. It had her mother's touch. When her and Abel moved here from the penthouse in the city, it was her mother, a former interior designer, that did the place up for them.

She walked to the closet and hung up her coat, pushing the door closed and releasing the handle quietly, trying to keep from making any noise that would indicate her homecoming. She stood there for a moment and took a deep breath, thinking about going to bed. There was no reason she could think of why she would have to talk to him tonight. All this could go away for one more evening. How much longer could she keep putting this off, she wondered. It was time to be a wife.

"God, please give me the strength," she whispered.

It was in the kitchen that she found him. He was sitting at the table with his arms folded in front of him, staring down at a cell phone as though it were a pest he had just seized.

Her standing there had not drawn his attention, so she made her presence known. "Hi there," she said.

He looked up and squinted—obviously tired. "Hey," he said, and smiled. He smiled at her. That felt good. For both of them.

"Of all the rooms in this house, why is it that I always find you in here?" she asked, walking more into the kitchen.

"It's pretty all-purpose," he said. "Easiest place to end up."

"I suppose that's true." She sat opposite of him at the table. "What are you doing?"

"I've been playing with this cell phone," he said. "I tried calling Dr. Corin earlier, but every time I punch in the number, it doesn't do anything."

"What do you mean?" She took the phone from the table. "Is it broken?"

"I guess so. If it ever worked in the first place. See, I punch in the number here, but it doesn't ring or anything. I don't even know how to get a dial-tone out of it."

"Cell phones don't have dial-tones," she said. "You have to push the 'send' button."

He took the phone from her and examined it again. "What 'send' button? I don't see a button with 'send' on it."

"No, it's the green button, right here. You punch in the number and then push the green button. When you're done with the call, you push the red button."

"What if I get a phone call?" he asked. "What do I push?"

"You push the green button," she said. "Actually, you could probably push anything and it would answer the call. Just don't push the red button or it will send your call directly to your voice mail."

"To my voice mail?" he asked.

Rebecca laughed. "Oh my goodness. We have a lot to teach you."

"Do I wear glasses?" he asked.

"I believe you had laser surgery to correct your vision."

"No kidding? Wow. I still feel like I need glasses." He set the phone down, keeping an eye on it as though it were going to leap from the table, and picked up the sandwich off of the plate next to him to take a bite.

"What are you eating?" she asked, watching a piece of the sandwich slip from between the slices of bread and plop on the table in front of him. "What is that? Is that an apple?"

"Yeah, it's an apple slice," he said. "It's tuna, mayonnaise, and apple slices. And I think I put some celery in there too. I sometimes put grapes in it, but we didn't have any grapes."

Rebecca screwed up her face. "Yuck."

"Oh, it's good," he said, tucking his bite between his teeth and cheek. "Want to try some? Here, I didn't use all my apple slices. I'll make you one." He got up from the table and went to the counter. "My mom always had the biggest trick getting me to eat my fruit. I like fruit; I just seem to gravitate more toward junk food for some reason."

Rebecca giggled. "I could see that."

"So anyway, I used to try some different combinations of food to incorporate fruit into my diet. I saw this movie where this guy was raving about this Waldorf sandwich, which was basically a fancy chicken salad, but it has some fruits like apples and grapes in it. I wondered how that would taste with tuna, and it turned out to be pretty good."

"I never knew any of this," Rebecca said.

"Really?"

"Yeah," she said. "You never talked about your childhood."

"Well," he started, "it's kind of all I remember these days." He turned around with her sandwich on a paper towel and handed it to her. "Here, try that."

She leaned down, putting her face almost on the table, looking at it sidewise and poked the topside piece of bread with her index finger.

Abel laughed. "Give me a break. Just try it."

She handled it with both hands and watched the guy across the table suspiciously as she bit into it. She chomped on it a few times before a discernable "Mm" hummed from her lips.

Abel chuckled and sat back down. "There. What'd I tell you?"

"That's not bad," she said, finishing her bite. "It kind of adds a sweet crunch to the fish."

"Add some lettuce and a glass of milk and I can get all the food groups in one sandwich."

Rebecca brushed the crumbs off her hands and found herself staring at Abel. She didn't mean to. It wasn't often she saw him smiling back at her and feeling like her company was enjoyed.

"What?" Abel asked her.

"What's your latest memory? What's the last thing you can remember?"

"Let's see," Abel wondered. "I remember this beautiful blonde woman trying one of my sandwiches and surviving."

She laughed. "No, I mean before…" She stopped, getting serious again. "Before the accident."

"I think I remember my nineteenth birthday," he said. "I don't remember my twentieth."

"So you still feel nineteen," she said.

"Actually, I don't," he chuckled. "I definitely feel older. This isn't the same body I left myself with. I mean, I'm fit for the most part, but I feel…I don't know…not well-taken-care-of."

"You drank a lot," she said.

He pursed his lips and merely nodded at that.

"Has it been tough adapting?"

He thought about that for a moment. "Yes. But I didn't feel like I belonged before all of this. Some of the feelings are the same—just in a different world."

"What did it feel like being nineteen?"

"Scary," he said. "Unsure of yourself. Not knowing what my purpose was, really."

"Were you in college?"

"I was thinking about dropping out. Jared said I did, but I don't remember that. He didn't really seem to want to talk about it, so I don't guess he really knows either. I wasn't a bad kid. I just didn't feel like I could do it on my own. I was feeling myself heading in the wrong direction and I wanted to come home and get my head straight before going back."

"What do you mean," she asked, "heading in the wrong direction?"

"I was hanging out with the wrong crowd," he said. "I mean, I knew what I was doing was wrong, but I was trying to feel accepted. Something I wasn't ever really getting from my parents either."

"I never knew your mom or dad."

"Yeah," Abel said, and then chuckled. "Neither did I, really. But that doesn't mean I don't miss them. That was a bit of a shock, too—waking up and finding your mom and your sister aren't alive anymore. My dad, who was more Jared's guardian than mine, died after Jared finished college."

"From the suicide," she said.

"Yeah, you knew that?" he asked.

Rebecca nodded. "Your mom died of cancer and your sister died during her pregnancy."

"Yeah, I still don't really know all the details about that. Well, the pregnancy anyway. Jared took care of my mom before she died. My parents were both pretty robotic. They were pretty strict on me and Jared and April. However, I never got any impression that their moral upstanding was grounded on anything. They said they were Christians and they probably were, but my dad gambled and my mom was a gossip. Dad was a Methodist and mom dragged us to Mass. The contrast in Christian beliefs made it all very confusing. After they got divorced, my dad didn't go to church anymore. I quit going to Catholic church when I got to college and joined a youth group." Abel stopped and smirked. "I'm sorry, I'm just rattling on. You've probably heard all of this a hundred times."

"No, I haven't," Rebecca said. "You never talked about your past. I knew hardly anything before your first number one song."

"Really?" he asked.

"Yeah, you were pretty closed about all of it."

"That's interesting," he said. And then he caught himself staring at her. For the first time since waking up from the accident, he felt like he had a friend.

Rebecca smiled in response. "What," she asked.

"How did we meet?" he asked her.

She turned her head down as her smile changed to somewhat embarrassment. "A mutual friend of ours introduced us," she said, "as it sometimes goes. We were both interns in the same publishing firm. Well, I was an intern. She had been on staff a few years. Anyway, we were at this publisher's seminar, and you were there too, but you were there for the music publishing end of things—said you were going to learn more about it so you could get out of it." And she laughed.

So did Abel. "It's funny, but I need to learn all this terminology over again."

"Okay, sorry," she said, and cleared her throat before she continued; "Anyway, we were sitting in on a particularly boring session. Actually, I didn't mind it so much, but you were bored and managed to talk me out of leaving to go get some dinner somewhere. I couldn't resist your charm. You were devilishly handsome, and I was a young naïve intern being approached by one of the biggest names in music publishing. So I obliged. We were married a year later."

Abel smiled. "And I've been a pain in the neck ever since."

Rebecca didn't say anything though her smile steadily diminished.

"I'm sorry," he said.

She shook her head. "You didn't know."

"Touché," Abel said. They both chuckled. "No, I meant that I'm sorry I said something that made you stop smiling. You have a beautiful smile. I miss it already." That of course earned her smile again. "Thank you," Abel complimented.

"It's why you married me," she said.

"Really?"

"Yeah, you said so you could see that smile every day for the rest of your life."

Abel smiled at that. "But I haven't." Rebecca wasn't looking at him anymore. He tried to say something reassuring. "I can see why I fell in love with you."

She sighed, and said politely, "I need to go to bed."

He nodded. "Me too."

"Thanks for the sandwich," she said as she stood.

He stood with her. "Rebecca?"

She stopped and looked at him.

Whatever it was Abel was going to say, he dismissed it. Perhaps he forgot, or wanted to say something encouraging and just didn't know what. "Goodnight," was all he could come up with.

She smiled for him once more and was away.

Jared stood over his eldest daughter, a teenager, watching her sleep. She wasn't yet old enough to drive, but all at once it seemed like he was watching her age right there in front of him. It felt like yesterday he was standing here over a bed much smaller, occupied by an equally smaller person, tucking in the parts of her body that dangled off the edge of the mattress.

Some things hadn't changed. He turned her body so that her leg and arm were back in the parameters of her slumber. She stirred at being moved with a slight groan, but remained asleep. Her dad carefully tucked the blanket around her snugly to prevent her from rolling off the bed again.

He checked on his other daughter and son and the one other boy of his he loved as his own before retiring to where his wife was sleeping. He quietly readied himself for bed in the adjacent bathroom and joined his wife, coming in under the covers behind her. Cuddling himself near, he wrapped his arm around her abdomen which stirred her awake.

"Hello," she said quietly, responding by pressing back against him.

"Did I wake you?" he asked.

"I haven't been asleep long."

"I love you," he said into her dark locks of curls.

"I love you," she replied. "How's Abel?"

"I didn't see him today. Rebecca said to say hello."

"How's she doing?"

"She's coping."

"The poor woman."

"The poor guy."

"Men," Emily lamented.

"Women," Jared countered in their bout of sarcasm.

"He was strangely well-behaved with the children the other day," she said. "I've never seen that side of him."

"He said he remembered you," Jared said. "His memory is pretty selective."

"We talked a little," she said softly, barely audible.

"You know," Jared started, "I really hate to admit it. And I hope you don't find me too terribly heartless for saying this. I'm starting to consider the accident a good thing. For him, anyway. I'm sorry for those families that lost their loved ones."

Emily just hummed. She was obviously teetering on falling asleep again. Jared leaned over her and kissed her on the temple. "Goodnight, love."

Abel flipped on the lights that surrounded the bathroom mirror and pulled down his lower eyelid, looking into his eyeball and pondering the miracle that was "laser surgery." He squinted, he widened his eyes, he looked left and right, and shrugged. Examining the age in his face from the last time he remembered looking at himself so closely, he smoothed out his cheeks and scratched his whiskers, frowning and smiling to see how many wrinkles formed.

Overall, he determined, his face wasn't as shapely. There was extra skin in some places it seemed like. He smoothed back his hair looking to see if any of it was thinning or had lost any of it since his teenage years.

It was then that he noticed the scar. He never would have seen it otherwise. It was well hidden just above where his hair might part on that side. He didn't recall ever seeing that scar before. It couldn't have been from the accident. Where might that have come from?

Chapter 4

"You were at one time disobedient to God, Paul says here in Romans chapter eleven in verse thirty. You right now are suffering from disobedience. Disobedience is a suffering. It is a pain we must endure; it is a burden we must carry if we are to know God's grace. We are all bound to disobedience so that we might know God's grace. If we were not disobedient, there would be no reason for it. But just as we are all imperfect before a perfect God, so we must embrace our imperfections if we are to seek that perfection that is found in God's grace. That's what Paul is saying here. We are allowed to have the choice to disobey so that we might also have a choice to be redeemed."

Abel was listening intently to the pastor's words. He was a passionate, bold speaker that couldn't stay still behind a pulpit. He walked the length of his stage area preaching from his Bible in one hand.

"Now, does that mean we should go out and sin if we are to know the grace of God? You don't have to. You have already sinned! God asks us to lead a life faithful to him, as it says in verse twenty-nine, 'for God's gifts and his call are irrevocable.' That means you have a responsibility to God and to His commands. However, don't be discouraged if you are not able to do it perfectly. You're going to sin. That's inevitable. The Bible says we are all sinners. That's just the way it goes. You are never going to rise above that. Your definitions of sin don't matter. Sin is our imperfection, and that's just the way we are.

"When you became a Christian, things weren't instantly going to become happy and cheerful and everything was going to figure itself out. But where there is sin, thankfully, there is grace to forgive us of that imperfection. If you are in Christ, you have that grace. Remember that verse we talked about last week examining Romans 10 when Paul said to confess with our mouths and we will be made unto salvation. Psalm 103 says God will take those confessions, He will throw them as far as the east is from the west, and He will remember them no more. There is forgiveness. All you have to do is ask for it."

Somewhere in another church in a different part of the city, Rebecca and her in-laws stood the aisle waiting patiently for the friendly Sunday-morning greetings to move toward the exit. Jared and Emily were both losing control of their children.

"Don't go far," Emily called after her escaping progeny. "We're going to go out to eat later."

"I didn't even think about inviting Abel to come," Jared said. "So many years of asking and his refusing to go that the thought never even crossed my mind."

"It's alright," Rebecca said. "He wasn't at home this morning anyway."

"He wasn't?"

"No," she said. "I got up and looked for him, but he wasn't home. He doesn't have anything going on so I don't know where he had to go. It's the first time he's left the house on his own free will since the accident."

"Why were you looking for him?" Emily asked.

Rebecca half-shrugged and seemed to avoid answering, but she soon confessed: "I was going to invite him to church."

Jared chuckled for some reason. "You were going to invite him to go to church?"

"Yeah, sure."

Jared stopped in their slow progression and turned to her. "So things are going well between you two?"

"Jared," Rebecca said sternly, "I've been inviting Abel to church every Sunday for a year now, despite the circumstances."

"I had no idea," he digressed. "You're welcome to join us for dinner by the way."

"Thanks, but I've got a lot of work I need to get done before tomorrow. You have no idea how behind I've gotten from all of this."

"Hey, look at that," Emily said.

"What?" Jared asked her. "Don't point."

"Isn't that Alex?"

"Trask?" He pivoted back and forth looking through the heads of people. "Yeah, so it is. He comes occasionally. It's a big church, so I don't always see him."

"Yes," Emily said, "but his wife used to come in with him and I don't see her anymore. I was just looking to see if she was there."

"I don't see her," Jared said.

Abel felt nauseated. He had flashbacks of waking up in an overturned vehicle, sick to his stomach. His head spun thinking about it as he stood now at the gate entrance of the address scribbled on his folded up piece of paper. He felt rather queasy, controlling his breaths to keep himself calm. The gate was open, but he left the car on the street anyway.

Just as he managed to convince his feet to move, his phone rang. It was relieving to have something draw his attention toward something else for a moment. He pulled the phone out of his coat pocket and looked at the display. Apparently it was "Greg" trying to call him. He pressed the power button switching the phone off, and stuck it back in his pocket. Onward he trekked up the driveway.

Abel bounced on his heels a couple of times as he waited for the doorbell to be answered. The door opened to a woman he didn't recognize. By her facial expression, the retreating smile, it was apparent that she recognized him.

"Mrs. Solis?" he asked her.

The woman didn't reply, leering at him with no more welcome than if he were a salesman.

"Are you Rachel?"

"I am," she said. "What do you want?"

"Um…" He got that sick feeling again. "I wanted to talk to you."

"About what?"

"About…" Abel stammered. "About your son. David."

Again, she was unresponsive.

"May I come in?"

She rolled her eyes and walked away from the door. "Gerald, come take the gentleman's coat and offer him a drink. Tell my husband that there is a visitor here for him."

The butler offered to take Abel's coat from him but Able refused and turned down his drink.

"I'm entertaining guests this afternoon," Mrs. Solis said as she walked into the living room, "otherwise I wouldn't have answered the door myself and the gate would have been closed to visitors. We shouldn't expect you stay long."

"No, of course not," Abel said. "I mean, I wouldn't want to keep you. And I just wanted to talk to the both of you."

"My husband will be down in a moment." Mrs. Solis walked to a table where wine was being chilled in a bucket of ice surrounded by wine glasses. She poured herself half a glass and consumed it rather quickly.

"Hello, who's here?" said Mr. Solis as he came in behind Abel. He stopped when Abel looked up at him. "Oh," he murmured. "It's you. Well what do you want here? Make it quick. Our guests will be arriving shortly."

"I'm sorry to be an imposition," Abel said. "I should have called, but…"

"Yesyesyesyes," Mr. Solis sputtered, stepping to his wife. "Enough of all of that. What do you want?"

"I just wanted to come and visit with you about David."

"What about David?" Mr. Solis asked. "We buried him in the ground. It's over. It's done."

"Yes, I know," Abel said. "But you're his surviving family. I just wanted to come by and say, face to face, how sorry I am for what happened. And I wanted to ask for your forgiveness."

"Uh huh," Mr. Solis said. "And you hoped that perhaps by coming over here to apologize that you might be able to get out of the settlement? Is that what it is?"

"No…"

"That's fine," Mr. Solis said. "It doesn't matter to me one way or the other. If you don't want to give us the money, then don't. Is that all?"

"No, no, not at all. No, that money is yours. I just felt that was fair. Well, I mean, it's not fair—it won't bring David back. It's just—the other families are getting settlements. I felt that you…"

"We didn't ask for a settlement," Mr. Solis said.

"I know you didn't. I just…"

"We weren't even going to take you to court."

"That's fine. I appreciate that. I just wanted…"

"Why are you doing this?" Mrs. Solis finally chimed in.

"I just want to say I'm sorry," Abel pleaded. "I wanted to apologize for putting your family through all of this. Forgive me. I'm sorry."

"Putting our family through all of what?" Mr. Solis said. "My son was an idiot. I loved my son, but he was an idiot. He couldn't even stay married to one woman. Or the one after that, for that matter. He knew what he was doing. He's dead because he's an idiot. Maybe, as you suggest, it's because you're an idiot. Frankly, I don't care! It's over, and that's the end of it. If he had been driving that car, and you were the one who died, I don't give a damn. If you got in the car with him in that condition, that makes you an idiot too. If you really want to make amends, just let it go. I release you of your conscience, or whatever it is I'm supposed to say. Just go on. Get out of here and don't bring this up again."

Abel stood with his hands in his pockets. His head would bow forward a few times, as though words were ready to come from him, but he had nothing.

"Go on!" Mr. Solis said again. "Go home!"

And that was the way to leave it, Abel decided. Defeated, he walked out the door and up the driveway, having to step aside and onto the grass when a car entered the gate and drove up the pavement. He cursed to himself when he forgot he locked his car and had to search his pockets for his keys. There he sat, watching as another car entered in the gate, swallowed by the high walls surrounding the private residence.

He gripped the steering wheel with all his might, losing his composure. Clasping his eyes shut, frustrated, he fought away his tears. When he opened his eyes again, he noticed a note had been put on his windshield tucked under the windshield wiper. He must not have noticed it until he got in the car.

The message was written on a white envelope. It said, "This is a warning. Leave it alone."

Rebecca sat at the grand piano at the head of the sanctuary looking at the black and white keys in front of her. She had a piano like it in her own living room, but couldn't honestly say she ever tried to see the same thing her husband saw when he played. It was funny at this moment; she didn't remember a piano having so many keys. It was so foreign to her. It was a different world. And perhaps it was in that she began to understand the environment Abel was living in since the accident. She felt responsible for making his recovery such an awkward situation for him.

Over the top of the piano, she saw a head merge from the other side of the pulpit. "I'm sorry to keep you waiting," the pastor said, dressed down from when she saw him in church earlier in the week. "We've been interviewing for the position of youth pastor."

"Yes, I've been reading about it," she said. "That's quite alright, Pastor Wayne. I don't usually do this. I know you have plenty going on."

"No, no, that's fine." The pastor motioned to the few stairs leading up to the stage. "Do you mind if we sit here? Is that too informal?"

"No, here would be fine." Rebecca got up from the piano bench and joined him.

"You know," Wayne started, "my wife and I started in a small midwest church in Nebraska. That was right after seminary. She was expecting our first child then. The nice thing about a small church like that is I was so in touch with the congregation. They could come over to our house anytime. We could sit and visit after the service. Everyone knew everybody. There was a good sense of unity. Now in a church this big, I sometimes forget how nice it is to forgo the head-pastor responsibilities and just be with the members again."

Rebecca smiled. "Thank you, pastor. I hope that you don't feel like I'm asking for any special treatment because of my husband's, you know, social standing or anything like that."

"Oh, hush. No. Nothing of the sort," he smiled back. "I'm sure what it is you want to talk about deals with the matter of your husband, is that correct?"

"Yes."

"Any improvements on his memory?"

"No, none," she said. "We've been talking a lot lately, and it's nice. I mean, I get the sense that he really wants to know about me. He's very attentive. It's something that I've never gotten before from him. I think what attracted me so much to him in the beginning was the thrill of having someone with such popular acclaim want to be with me. You know; he'd call me up and ask me to dinner. He would invite me to the parties he was going to. That sort of thing."

"Sure," the pastor said.

"However, I don't know that I ever felt a real sense of belonging, you know? When I look back on it, there was no attention on me. He didn't ask me about my interests, he didn't ask me about my work or about my family. At the same time, he didn't really talk about his. We were just there for the sake of each other and that was it. It wasn't even just to have someone to talk to because we didn't talk. Even though I felt that need of companionship was being met by him, it really wasn't."

"I can understand that," he said, listening.

"But now, it's completely different," she said. "We talk. And he talks about his childhood because that's the only thing he remembers. He remembers high school and grade school and life at home, and it's great. He has dreams and ambitions which I didn't even know he had before. I guess I just took it for granted that winning awards and making lots of money was his accomplishing goals."

The pastor chuckled.

"But pastor, even most of all—and this has been an answer to prayer—he's a Christian."

"Is he?"

"Yes. Apparently he was very much a Christian when he was a teenager. Something happened to him in college—which he accredits to hanging out with the wrong crowd, but he says he doesn't remember—that made him turn away from Christianity and become the person that I knew him as. Or know him as. Or whatever. I knew from his brother that he had a pretty moral upbringing, but I didn't know he was a Christian."

"How is your relationship with his brother?"

"Well," she started, "you know that it was Jared and Emily that brought me to become a Christian last year."

"Yes."

"Or a little more than a year now. Anyway, they've been great in helping me along with my spiritual maturity. Ever since becoming a Christian, it just opened my eyes up to the world around me. As soon as I accepted Jesus into my life, I saw how fake the world was I was living in. I saw how unhappy my marriage really was. I saw how unproductive I was in my work and everything else. Honestly, for a while, I wanted to go back to not being a Christian. I just couldn't take how tragic my world had become."

"That's understandable," Pastor Wayne acknowledged. "And you know what? The Bible talks about that."

"Really?"

"Yes. The philosopher in Ecclesiastes says with much wisdom comes much sorrow; the more knowledge, the more grief. Acts 26:18 says, 'To open their eyes, and to turn them from darkness to light, and from the power of Satan unto God, that they may receive forgiveness of sins, and inheritance among them which are sanctified by faith that is in me.' I'm sorry; I'm a King James scripture reader."

"That's alright," Rebecca smiled.

Pastor Wayne chuckled too. "Some of the deacons don't like it. I suppose I'm still a little old fashioned. Anyway, the king of Babylon also acknowledged this to Daniel in the Old Testament, before we had this atonement for our sins. He said, 'Of a truth it is that your God is a God of gods, and a Lord of kings, and a revealer of secrets.' There is truth in that old scripture which has since become a famous saying: 'You will know the truth, and the truth will set you free.' When you became a Christian, your eyes were opened to the truth. It's not that it made your marriage unhappy. Your world didn't become a tragedy. Your marriage was already unhappy, and the life around you was unfulfilling. You just didn't realize it until you accepted Christ into your life and became a 'new creation' as it says in Colossians. Second Corinthians chapter five says that through his forgiveness, through that grace of His that we accept, we no longer live for ourselves."

"I truly believe all of that," Rebecca said. "That's exactly what I felt. It was a difficult transition."

"It is," the pastor said. "But you're okay with it now?"

"Oh, yes," she said. "I'm reading my Bible and praying every day."

He smiled. "Good girl."

"But I can't say it's easy every day."

"No, and it won't be. But I want you to consider this," he said, having to clear his throat. "When you became a Christian, your world was new to you. It was a startling contrast, was it not?"

"Right," she said.

"Consider then what Abel must be feeling with this gap in his life of all that has happened."

She nodded. "He really is a completely different person."

"I'm sure he is."

"And you know something," she said, looking away from him for a moment, and then making eye contact with him again, "I don't think I want him to have his memory back."

"Why?" the pastor asked. "Because it's the easiest way to deal with your struggling marriage?"

"I never thought about it that way before, but I suppose that could be true. It's really because I like him more as this person than I did as the other person. Is it wrong to feel that way? I mean, does that make me a bad wife? I have a lot of thoughts like this—even that my prayers somehow brought about this accident. Sometimes I feel like since I became a Christian, I'm more aware of my own inadequacies. I believe that God has a meaning and a purpose for my life, but I can't help but feel that I don't amount up to certain things. I don't know how else to say that." Pastor Wayne was about to say something before Rebecca had another thought jump into her head. "I suppose one example would be by saying I feel wronged by my husband, the way I've been neglected our whole marriage, but I can't blame him anymore than I can blame myself."

"You know what I think?" the pastor asked.

"What's that?"

"I think you haven't forgiven yourself yet."

"Forgiven myself?" Rebecca quirked. "You mean I haven't forgiven Abel yet."

The pastor shook his head. "No, I mean you haven't forgiven yourself."

"What do you mean, forgive myself?"

"When you became a Christian, you accepted God into your life. Correct?"

"Right."

"Have you yet considered yourself accepted by God?"

Rebecca thought a moment. "I don't know."

"You know, Rebecca," the pastor began, "Christianity can come with its ups and downs like the rest of life does. However, it's not a feeling. It's not something that you just wake up and feel some days and don't the others. It's an attitude. It's an approach to the way you live your life. If you cannot forgive yourself, if you can't have an attitude of being forgiven, how are you going to forgive others? If you cannot learn to forgive yourself, you are placing yourself in a position higher than God."

Rebecca screwed up her face. "A place higher than God?" He nodded. "How is that?"

"If all you think is that by stopping a good or bad habit, or overcoming a bad thought or deed, that this makes you a better person or a better Christian, you are actually saying you are bigger than God—you supersede his grace. But no human being can. In Ephesians chapter two, we are told that by grace we are saved through faith, not of ourselves. It is a gift of God so that we don't try comparing ourselves to other people."

"But how do I forgive myself?" she asked. "I don't understand that."

"That," Pastor Wayne said, "is something you're going to have to find out for yourself. But I will tell you this—when you became a Christian, you became complete. There is no next-level of spirituality. God will not love you more or less than He does now. You're there. Now you must learn to accept it. And live it."

Abel wasn't paying much attention when the door swung open and hit him in the chest. He managed to protect the flowers he was carrying from being smashed against him. "Oh, I'm so sorry," was the apology of the hurried woman coming from the other side.

"It's alright," Abel said. "It's not every day that I get an apology from anyone."

"Abel," the woman said. That's all she said. But she said it with such familiarity in her reaction that he felt like he should have also known who she was. He didn't recognize her. She was the wife of his lawyer, Alexander Trask. He hadn't met her before, at least since the accident, so he had no reason to know her. She was dressed down in gray sweats and a windbreaker, her dark hair pulled back, face plain without makeup. Her hair was a different color then it was following the trial, but not that he would have realized that. The two locked eyes.

"Do we know each other?" he asked. This type of question never got any easier.

The woman stood for a spell, the same look frozen on her face. She looked at the flowers in his hand and back to his face before she finally responded, "No, we don't." With her arms loaded of files, she retreated quickly to a black car and got in the backseat before it pulled away from the curb.

An odd exchange, he puzzled. The publishing firm he walked into was where his wife worked. He was directed to the floor her office was on, but she wasn't in.

"My name is Alice," her secretary said to him. "You probably don't remember me, but we've met before."

Abel smiled. "I'm sure I won't forget it this time, Alice."

She was a giggly little thing with what he guessed to be a Virginian accent.

"Do you know when Rebecca will be back?"

"She didn't specify," Alice replied, "but she did say she'd be back in before I went home. Do you want me to leave her a message? Oh, are those for her?"

"Yes, it was all the tulips they had." Abel handed her the three wrapped in tissue paper. "Must be out of season. It was just one of those little corner places."

"Oh, they're beautiful!" Alice exclaimed. "She'll love them. I'll put these in some water for her and put them on her desk. Do you want to write her a note?"

"No, that's alright," Abel said. "Just tell her they're from me."

Leaving the building the same way he came in, another face he couldn't remember stopped him and claimed to recognize him. "Abel?" he said. "Abel West?"

"Yeah, do we know each other?" Abel asked.

"It's me! It's Trevor! We went to college together."

"Hey, Trevor. How are you?"

"Oh, you know. Same old. I work with your wife, you know."

"You don't say."

"Yeah, different department, but I see her every once in a while. You know, all the floors are open in there."

"Right."

"Hey, remember the tech game from a few months back? Before Thanksgiving? You bet me and lost. Do you remember that? Of course, you don't remember that. Hey, you owe me a hundred bucks, you know."

"No, I don't know," Abel retorted.

"Yeah. And I even bought you a drink since then. Come on. Pay up, bro!" He threw his shoulder into him all playful-like.

Abel wasn't so flattered by the exchange of camaraderie. "What college did we go to together?"

"What?" Trevor smirked. "You mean you forgot that too? Come on. How far back does that memory of yours go?"

"Before college apparently," Abel said.

Trevor was able to pick up on the sarcasm. He was hesitant, but he gave his answer: "You know, we went to Tech together."

"Which Tech?" Abel pressed.

"What do you mean which Tech? You know. Tech. Virginia Tech."

"Really?" Abel asked. "To the best of my knowledge, I've never lived in Virginia."

Trevor lost that giddy smile of his.

"And I know I didn't attend a Tech college."

Okay, so Trevor was caught in his scheme to con a hundred bucks out of Abel West. But he didn't stand defeated. He threw his shoulder into him again and patted him on the shoulder. "I'm just messin' with you, man. I just wanted to see if that head of yours still worked, you know? So how are things going?"

Abel smiled and arched his eyebrows. "They're going." He walked away.

Behind him, he could still hear Trevor mutter, "Yeah, see you later," and added, "jerk."

Abel spun back around. "I'm a jerk? *I'm* a jerk? You just lied to get a hundred bucks out of me!" But the arguing didn't do any good. After stabbing him in the back, Trevor slinked out of view. Abel shook his head and moved on. No sense in arguing with a fool.

Chapter 5

Abel didn't know much about the family history with psychiatrist Dr. Ellis Corin. All he knew was he trusted him. He had not written one book on any case study, so Abel felt reassured that he wasn't going to be Dr. Corin's next money-making venture.

The lack of publications didn't make his credentials any less prestigious. Dr. Corin was one often relied upon for duplicate or follow-up research and a second opinion in any given field related to psychology. He was among a board of doctors who approved certain texts admissible in high schools and colleges. A native of Canada, he once served on the board of the Canadian Psychological Association and helped launch the Enhancing Interdisciplinary Collaboration in Primary Health Care initiative. However, he was bothered by his country's politics and battled against governmental interference with private practice—which made him increasingly unpopular in certain circles.

Caring only for the advancement of psychiatry, he moved to the states and did some work with the American Psychological Association. He resigned after a short time saying that the APA embraced too many secular ideals without being scientific about many of them. He also served with the Association for Transpersonal Psychology and never quite shared with anyone why he renounced his membership there. Perhaps, like with the APA, there were too many conflicts with his personal beliefs about how psychology should be conducted.

After his stints sitting on a few boards, he returned to teaching and psychiatry. His practice as of late has been mostly private, and he preferred it that way. Too much chair-sitting in various organizations was his way of gaining social acclaim. He wasn't thinking about that anymore. He felt like the most work he could do was one-on-one—whether that be in his office or the classroom.

Affiliated with one of the local Universities, Corin taught classes to students reaching for their masters degrees, specifically in the areas of psychology and psychiatry.

"I want you to consider something," Corin said from the head of the classroom. "Would you rather feel alone and unloved in the world, or would you rather feel inadequate and disrespected?" After a brief spell, the students began mumbling to one another. "How many of you would rather feel alone and unloved? Raise your hands."

The right half of the classroom raised their hands.

"Okay, now, how many of you would rather feel inadequate and disrespected? Raise your hands."

The left half of the classroom raised their hands.

Some students chuckled at the difference in the responses.

"You laugh about it," Corin chuckled, "but you have no idea how much truth you just displayed by answering that question. A lot of you asked me at the beginning of the semester why I had the guys sit on one side of the classroom and the girls sit on the other. The answer is right there. Men would rather be alone in the world than feel inadequate and disrespected, and women are the other way around. Women really want to be loved and cherished. Every woman in this room raised her hand."

Corin turned and started writing on the board. "The idea that men and women are equal is absolutely false. Men and women are not equal. They are night and day from each other. They behave differently, react differently, they emote different things, their bodies function differently, they repress and recall in different ways."

He stopped writing and stood in front of them again. "True, men and women both might experience a fear of being undesired. But it doesn't stop there. You have to look at how they feel they are undesired. Women, when you look down on your boyfriends or husbands, he feels disrespected. Men, when you don't talk or listen to your girlfriends or wives, they feel abandoned. They are both feeling undesired, but felt in different ways. For those of you looking at going into psychiatry, don't ever consider men and women as equal."

It wasn't clear exactly how long Dr. Corin had been a Christian. He hadn't always incorporated such a moral approach to his sessions. For as long as he'd been in this office, so were his Christian beliefs, evident by various framed verses hanging on the walls and perched on shelves and his desk. Abel was referred to him, but he preferred him.

"That pastor's words have been swirling around in my head ever since," Abel said, sitting comfortably in the plush, deep-red leather chair. "I can't seem to get them out of my mind."

"What about them specifically," Dr. Corin asked, "do you think made them target you?"

"It's exactly what I've been going through," he said. "Dealing with matters of forgiveness. It's interesting, but I don't even know what I'm asking for forgiveness for. I don't remember any of it. I just know that I'm wrong, like the pastor said. I've done something wrong whether I'm aware of it or not; we all have. The problem is—and this is what makes the pastor's sermon even more haunting to me—is that asking for forgiveness hasn't been working."

"What do you mean?"

"I mean that I ask for it, but I don't receive any of it. No one is willing to give it to me. It's like as much as I'm willing to want to let go of this, no one else is. And it's not just the families I told you about. It's not just the feeling I get from my wife. It's indirect every-day things. It's Greg taking me to the bar and buying me a drink. It's unrolling the weekend newspaper to read another article or accusation about this whole thing. It's the conversation I overheard between those couple of guys at the café the other day."

"Tell me about that," Corin said.

"Well," Abel started, "you know, since the accident has been this whole new world to me. It's cell phones and computers and em-pee-three players and all this personal gadgetry. So I took a day to just wander around and get acquainted with stuff. When it came time for lunch, I sat down at this little café…"

GUY 1: "So what do you think about this whole thing with Abel West?"
GUY 2: "Who?"
GUY 1: "Abel West. You know, the songwriting big-shot who lost his memory in that accident."
GUY 2: "Oh, right, right. I think he's faking it, entirely."
GUY 1: "Really? Why do you think that?"
GUY 2: "Come on! Look what he's getting out of. He could spend the rest of his life in jail for getting behind the wheel of a car under the influence. Witness testimony says they saw him get drunk that night. But if he gets thrown in prison, he loses his whole life and all his money. Would you plead ignorance to keep from losing all that? I sure would. I'd do cartwheels in the nude and sit in a pile of my own dung to plead insanity for that."
GUY 1: "I hear a lot of stuff about it, but I don't really know which way to lean. I mean, the guy's gotta be awfully insensitive to just say he doesn't remember it and manage to pull off stupidity for the rest of his life."
GUY 2: "Wouldn't be that hard. You've done it before."
GUY 1: "How do you know?"
GUY 2: "Two weeks ago when we were celebrating Gary's promotion. We were at that strip club. Did you tell your wife about that?"
GUY 1: "No, she figures we just went out to the bars."
GUY 2: "Right. And she still doesn't know yet, does she?"
GUY 1: "That's different. She didn't ask me about it and I didn't kill anyone."
GUY 2: "Oh, give me a break! If she asked you, would you tell her the truth?"

GUY 1: *"Sure, why not?"*

GUY 2: *"Whatever! You'd lie through your teeth! You're lying to me right now!"*

GUY 1: *"Yeah? How do you know?"*

GUY 2: *"And you know that if you did tell the truth, someone would die because of it, and that someone would be you."*

GUY 1: *(just laughs)*

GUY 2: *"A lie is a lie is a lie. You're no better than this Abel guy."*

GUY 1: *"Yeah, but that's if he's lying."*

GUY 2: *"He's lying. But you know, he probably didn't forget about fifteen years of his past. He probably just forgot about last night, you know? I've been that drunk before. A friend of mine was at that party and she said she saw him drinking. That wasn't water in his glass. 'Put me on the witness stand,' she said to me, 'I'll tell them what I saw.' But they were all drunk at that party. Who are you going to believe?"*

"Now, I know this guy didn't know a friend at that party," Abel said. "He had to ask who Abel West was when the conversation started." Corin was trying to hold back his laughter. "Now I'm everyone's lab specimen when they talk about lying. Or they say I'm faking it to get out of my guilty conscience. I'm bombarded with constant reminders of my past. Some people have even been taking advantage of my memory loss, or putting it to the test to see if it's really real. I even got a note put on my car."

"A note put on your car?" Corin asked.

"Yeah," Abel said. "I was trying to apologize to the Solis's, and I got a warning on my car that said to leave it alone."

"Did you tell the authorities about that?" Corin asked.

"No, I didn't know what it meant," Abel said. "I had no idea who it might have come from."

"Did your lawyer advise you to apologize to the Solis family? Seems kind of risky."

"No, I did that on my own."

"Well, not knowing if the note was friendly or hostile, I'd still say leaving it alone is something to consider."

"Honestly, no one else is more haunted by this than I am. This memory-loss thing is not a cop-out for me. It doesn't make me any less guilty or less responsible for my dishonesty."

"I'm glad you're mature enough to consider that," Dr. Corin said.

"I know that what I did was wrong," Abel said, "but I don't know what to do to make it right. How do I move on from this when no one will let me? How do I find grace when none of it is given?"

"Have you asked God for forgiveness?" Corin asked intently.

"Plenty of times. I'm in my Bible every day. And like I said, I don't even remember what it is that I'm asking forgiveness for. I just know that I should."

Corin was nodding. "Are you familiar with second Corinthians 12:9?"

"I'm sure I've heard of it," Abel shrugged, "or read it before, but I'm not sure."

"My grace is sufficient for you."

"What does that mean?" Abel said.

"His grace is sufficient," Corin said. "It's all you need. It's not important for you to earn everyone else's forgiveness—it is God's grace that will suffice. And He has told us when we ask for it, we shall receive it. Now, that doesn't mean that we shouldn't also ask others for forgiveness. Even the Lord's prayer says 'forgive us our debts as we forgive or debtors.' So we are to ask other's forgiveness when we do wrong—that in according to God's will for us. And then we also forgive those who ask for forgiveness. However, if they don't give it to you, God's grace is enough."

"But how do I move on from this when I'm surrounded by reminders everywhere?"

"The Bible doesn't say anything about taking our memories away," Corin said. "That's just part of learning. That's part of dealing with our transgressions. In the rest of that verse from second Corinthians, Paul says, 'I will boast all the more gladly about my weaknesses, so that Christ's power may rest on me. That is why, for Christ's sake, I delight in weaknesses, in insults, in hardships, in persecutions, in difficulties. For when I am weak, then I am strong.'"

Abel nodded his affirmations, but Dr. Corin could still see a lack of hope in his downcast eyes.

"Abel," Corin started, "do you realize how blessed you are? There are many people that are haunted by their pasts. Your wife may very well be one of them. You, on the other hand, have no recollection of most of your past. Not only has God forgiven you for all of that stuff, he's removed the memory of it for you as well. You are being given a second chance. The question is: what are you going to do with it?"

"That's the thing, Doc," Abel said. "Whether I know my past or not, I'm still haunted by it. I can't get over it. I'm having to defend myself and I don't know what from. Even my brother can't tell me much about my life after high school because we were so far apart until just a few years ago. I have this scar behind my hairline I don't know what it's from. There's just so many things I don't know that I wish I did."

Dr. Corin sighed and crossed his arms. "Do you really want to know them?"

"I want to know what you think I should do."

"My recommendation is to let it go," Dr. Corin said. "Forget about it and move on. If your memory heals itself and you start to remember these missing parts of your past, then so be it. If not, just let it go."

Abel leaned forward and rested his elbows on his knees. "What if I want to know?"

"There are ways," Dr. Corin said. "Hypnotism: find out what you've repressed in your subconscious. Although I don't have the expertise to do that for you."

"I'm having a hard time trusting certain people. What can you do for me?"

"I can start by digging up your medical and other personal records. And we can go from there. I'll have to have you sign a permission statement for me to do that."

"I'll do it."

"I'm not a private investigator, Abel. It's not going to be a thorough retelling of your lost years."

"I'm reaching for anything here. Anything at all."

"I just want you to know," Dr. Corin said, "and this is me speaking to you as a friend of the family and not as your doctor, that I'm against the idea of you doing this. You can't change the past and we don't know what's going to happen tomorrow. All we have is this moment right now. Change your life by making the most of now. I don't know what you think you're going to accomplish by doing this."

Abel shook his head. "I don't know either."

Chapter 6

Music was once heard every day in the West household. After Rebecca and Abel got married, she would often sit there at the baby grand with him in their high-rise penthouse while he serenaded her with impromptu love song. That was how he proposed to her. It wasn't long after they got married that the piano playing became less and less. The private concerts were no more, and Abel would only compose in the office he set up for himself—a small studio with several piano keyboards and computers to assemble his songs.

When they moved out of the city and into this luxurious home, Abel got something he always wanted to have but never had room for—a full-sized grand piano. It rarely got played. He would retreat to his study to compose where other ears couldn't hear.

That's why it took Rebecca by surprise to walk into a house full of music. It echoed off the ceiling and circulated the enclosure, sounding like it was coming from everywhere. The music was untamed, unrestrained, played to its fullest. She recognized the melody. Something classical. Though the sound of music felt like something new.

She walked into the living room and saw Abel there at the piano playing away. The sight was refreshing and somewhat shocking all at the same time. A tingle inside of her stirred an emotion she couldn't place, erupting to the music and filling her mind with questions.

Abel stopped playing when she came around the corner. "Oh, hello," he said. "I'm sorry; I didn't hear you come in."

"Sorry to have stopped you," she said. Abel didn't mind. He began playing a slower, softer melody. "What were you playing?"

"Beethoven," he said.

"I heard a rumor that you forgot how to play the piano."

"I was bluffing," he said. "I started playing the piano in middle school. It isn't just something you forget. I just didn't want to work for those guys."

"You should be careful," she advised. "If someone knew that, they could perceive you as faking your amnesia."

"Do you think I'm faking my amnesia?" he asked.

The question caught her off guard. As she thought about it, she realized she couldn't answer yes or no. "I don't know what to think," she said safely.

Abel nodded and continued playing.

"Thank you for the flowers the other day," she said.

He smiled, still looking at his keys.

"I wonder," she said, coming closer to the piano; "Why would you tell someone you forgot how to play the piano?"

"I can't read music," Abel said. "I never have been able to. I play by ear. I can listen to a song once and know it instantly. If I have learned to read music, it's been since college. The day I faked my ability to play, they were asking me to read something I couldn't."

"Is that all it was?" she asked.

He shrugged and looked at the keys again. "I don't know what they expect of me."

"What who expects of you?"

"Anyone," he replied. "Come here. Sit down." He scooted over on the piano bench. Rebecca was hesitant, but she came over and joined him, consciously not sitting to close. He began to play a soft melody and accompanied it in singing.

When the world weighs me down
And everybody tells me
What I'm supposed to be
When I'm lost in the crowd

GABRIEL PETER

Everyone's around but
There's no one around for me

When my way is not enough
Show me where I'm supposed to go from here
When I'm reaching out for love
Take my hand and tell me you are near

When I don't understand
Am I forcing this to happen
The way I want things to be
When I don't have command
And I'm tossing in the harbor
Before I'm even out to sea
When I have nothing left to show
More than ever I need to know

When my way is not enough
Show me where I'm supposed to go from here
When I'm reaching out for love
Take my hand and tell me you are near

"That's beautiful," Rebecca commented. "Did you just write that?"

"Just today, yes."

"What's it called?"

"I don't really have a title," he said. "I suppose I'd call it *When*. It's not quite finished yet."

"What are you going to do with that?"

He shrugged. "I don't know. Give it to Greg, maybe."

"I don't know a Greg."

"That's alright."

"It's different from all the other stuff you've written."

"I know," he said. "I've only heard a few songs of mine actually, but I know it's different." Rebecca lingered at him for a moment. Abel could feel her gaze. It made him smile. "What?" he asked.

"Nothing," she said. "It's just that you haven't sung to me in a very long time."

"I'm sorry for that," he said.

She shook her head somewhat. "You know, I completely feel the sympathy in your apology. But at the same time, you don't really know what it is you're apologizing for."

"That's true. I don't."

She sighed through her nose and looked down at the piano keys. They were the same black-and-white's she was looking at in the church. They were just as foreign to her, even in a place as familiar as her home. She remembered the words the pastor said to her and turned to say something to Abel. They met each other by saying the other's name at the same time.

Abel snickered. "I'm sorry, you go ahead."

"No, you first," she said.

He opened his mouth to speak, hesitated, and finally was able to ask, "Do you want to go to dinner with me sometime?"

She smiled. "I was just about to ask you the same thing."

Perhaps it was the low lighting. Maybe it was the classy restaurant. It could have been in the fact that Abel and Rebecca West were smiling together—an uncommon disposition for the both of them in the same place at the same time. Whatever the distraction, no one seemed to recognize them. Abel enjoyed it. He could sit and visit with someone in public and not have to be questioned about current events.

For the most part, Abel's name had begun to dwindle in the news. The accident probably wouldn't have been so heavily publicized in the first place if it wasn't also for this amnesia that resulted from it—a recognized but rare after-effect. Also the death of rising star Darrel Druse added to the hype. In circles that Abel used to include himself, he was often met with hostile stares. He didn't feel like he could ever belong there anyway. Not again.

He was building for himself a new life. At the same time, he was reviving an old one; spending time with his brother, sister-in-law, his nieces and nephews, and his wife.

"Because I have allergies," Rebecca responded to his question.

"Really?" Abel quirked with a smile. "Cats too?"

"Yes, I'm allergic to cats too. I love animals—I just can't be around them."

"And yet your favorite cartoon is still *Heathcliff*?"

Rebecca nodded and chuckled.

"That's interesting," Abel said. "Well I wondered why we had so much space but didn't at least have a dog."

"Part of it was the penthouse," she said. "We couldn't have pets up there anyway. I think when we moved to the house, we could have had a dog since it was a lot more open. But you never asked and I didn't say."

"We haven't been on the best of speaking terms for a while I take it," Abel said.

Rebecca smiled somewhat and shook her head as she took a sip of her wine.

"I'm wondering," Abel said.

"What?" she replied.

"Are you as guarded as you are because you're still afraid of me? Or are you guarded because you think there was something about yourself that made me turn away from you before?"

"What do you mean?" she asked.

He chuckled trying to find a better way to word that. "Are you guarded because of me or are you insecure? The obvious answer is that it has something to do with me. I'm sitting here and I'm looking at a positively beautiful woman, very poised and seemingly confident, surrounded by success and support from others, yet you're shielding yourself from something. And I'm wondering what it was that made you that way."

"How far back do you want to go?"

"What's the first thought that came to mind when I asked you?"

She smiled, but it wasn't really a smile. "Five years old."

"What happened when you were five?"

"My dad cheated on my mom."

"I'm sorry."

She shook her head. "She was pregnant at the time. And lost the baby probably because of the stress. She was so sad. It was devastating—to me as well as to her. To this day, I've never seen her cry like that."

"And even at five, you knew everything that was going on with your father?"

She nodded.

"I'm sorry," he said again.

"You didn't know me yet."

"I know. I'm just sorry someone would do that to you."

Rebecca looked at him. "Abel…"

"What?" he asked.

She shook her head. "Nevermind."

"No. What? What is it?"

"Why this sudden interest in me?" she asked. "Eventually you're not going to find me interesting anymore. Just like before. We'll just stop talking and have this professional little relationship like we did years before your accident."

"I don't want that to happen," Abel said. "You're my wife. I don't know—I just feel this responsibility to care for my wife."

"But you don't know me."

"You're right, I don't," he said. "That's why I asked you out to dinner. I want to get to know you."

"I don't want you to feel obligated toward me."

"Rebecca, obligation has nothing to do with it. I can't expect to feel in love with you all the time. I'm not going to wait to wake up from my amnesia and suddenly love you again or whatever my feelings were before the accident. If I've told you I love you, if I've made vows and a commitment toward you, I've got to hold on to that. It's my responsibility. And it's because I love you that I do it."

She looked at him with somewhat of a furrow in her brow. "You're nineteen."

He shrugged. "I suppose in some ways, yes."

"And you're more mature than most thirty-four year-olds I know."

That made him laugh. "Well I'll take that as a compliment." She smiled a little bit. He added, "I made a pretty bright kid. I just seem to be a stupid adult."

"Are you finished?"

"With my dinner? I think so, yes. Are you?"

She nodded. "Let's go for a walk."

They could see each other's breath against the night air as they walked through the dimly lit park dividing the streets that ran on all four sides. The traffic was only heavy on one avenue. Despite the world that continued to move around them, the couple felt alone together as they walked laps around the park area, hands in their coat pockets, talking and sharing.

"Neither one of us wanted to have any kids," she said. "We were both too wrapped up in our careers to want a family. I sometimes wonder if you only married me because I got pregnant and you felt it was your obligation to do so."

"You did?" he asked.

"I had an abortion, but we got married anyway. You felt it was your solemn duty as a man or something. I don't know."

"I remember feeling that way when my sister got pregnant," Abel said. "The guy didn't stick around. I didn't even know who he was. I just hated that a guy would do that to a girl and leave her."

"There was a point in our marriage," Rebecca continued, "where we were very comfortable with each other, very much in love, and decided a family was a good idea. I got pregnant and had a miscarriage."

"I'm sorry," he said.

"You were there for the first," she said. "You weren't there for the second."

"You had two miscarriages?"

"The doctors considered the possibility that I wouldn't successfully be able to have children. One doctor even suspected it was because of the abortion. You know," she said, getting off the pregnancy issue, "we never really fought. It was like we were too busy to fight. But we were also too busy to pay attention to one another. After a while, you weren't so attracted to the idea of being a family man anymore. You were back at your meetings and your parties and hanging out with the guys. I drowned myself in work, but under the surface when I was by myself, I was incredibly depressed. I got hooked on prescription drugs to numb the feelings I had every day. Emily took notice of my depression and started inviting me to church. As the story goes, I got pretty cleaned up and became a Christian."

"Was I indifferent toward you about that?" Abel asked.

"I didn't really sense that you had an opinion about it," she commented. "I didn't get a reaction out of you one way or the other. Honestly, I think I had selfish reasons about going to church at first. I thought it might upset you. I wanted you to pay attention to me somehow—even if it meant yelling at me. But you didn't. There was just nothing there. I started inviting you to church, just about every Sunday, but you would never come."

"I'm going now."

"So I've heard."

The two had veered more into the park to be away from the streets now.

"I had a new relationship. It was a relationship unlike anything I had ever experienced. I was in love with Jesus. I was a Christian. I was very happy and at the same time very sad. You got into a relationship yourself. I was never able to prove it, but suspected you were having an affair with another woman."

"Really," Abel said, matter-of-factly.

"Yes," Rebecca replied. "I'm sorry," she said. "I don't mean to be throwing all this stuff at you at once. I mean…" She sighed, and kind of grumbled to herself. "I'm not doing very well with this myself. I mean, you're still Abel. But you're not. You know?"

"Do you want to stop talking about it?" he asked. "I don't mean to push you."

"Do you want to stop?"

"I have to face these things," he said. "I just don't want this to be uncomfortable for you."

"All of this is uncomfortable for me."

"I'm sorry," he said.

She wanted to tell him not to apologize, especially since he didn't know what he was apologizing for. It was on the tip of her tongue. But she didn't say it.

"Did you know who it was I was having an affair with?" Abel asked.

"Like I said, I didn't know for sure."

"Did you have your suspicions?"

"I did."

"Who do you think I was sleeping with? Do I know her?"

"Is it that important?" she asked.

"If it's someone I've been in contact with, I want to know who it is I'm hurting."

"I don't know if you have," she said. "But you know her husband. It was Alexander Trask's wife."

The air dotted with Abel's occasional breath suddenly became very still as his breath caught in his throat.

"I should have known better," Rebecca said, "since she was the one that introduced us."

"Do you think he knew?" he was finally able to ask.

"I don't know," she said. "I figured if he did know it was you sleeping with his wife, he wouldn't have represented you in court.

Then again, he might have represented you to keep his wife off the witness stand. I'm not sure."

"So that's when we started counseling?"

"I told you I'd divorce you if we didn't get counseling. Which we had a big argument about—saying that I couldn't prove anything if I did try to get a divorce. It was probably our only big fight. But to save face, you agreed to the counseling. In the meantime, you continued to be out a lot. I don't know if you were still in the affair or what. I was quietly communicating with others about getting a divorce. I just didn't see our marital problems being reconciled. And then you were in that accident. And that brings us up to now."

"Wow," Abel commented.

"I know so very little about you," she said. "I knew little of your past and little of what you did behind my back. I just don't know what to think, Abel. I don't know how to take all of this."

He stopped her and pulled her around to face him. They stood there in the middle of the park to sounds of distant traffic horns, bus engines, and city noise, looking into one another's eyes.

"Rebecca," he started, "is this why you won't let me apologize for any of this?"

"You didn't know," she said.

"You're right, I didn't know," he said. "You have no idea how much sense that makes. I truly believe that we wrong each other because we just lack empathy. We just have no idea what the other person is thinking or feeling or going through. Regardless of whether or not I can remember what I put you through, it still happened because I wasn't aware of it. And it's still my fault. I'm sorry."

"I'm sorry, too," she whispered.

"I really want things to change," he said. "I sincerely do."

"I do, too."

They looked at each other for a long while, and then embraced. She held on to him. And hoped for the best.

I wish I said the words I didn't say
We can't go back now anyway
Would I have said the things I'd later
Wish I'd kept inside
I wish I knew the things I know now
We can't go back there anyhow
Would I have opened up
In ways I'd later try to hide
You're still with me
More than you can know

    The woman sat in the small booth at the bus stop but it wasn't a bus she was waiting for. She didn't want to go home and she didn't want to leave. Her hands in her pockets fingering at the emptiness there, she rocked back and forth, arms tensed clinging tightly to her self. She looked down the street in the direction the few cars traveled on her side. The street was rather still this night.
    Each breath she breathed formed clouds hanging in front of her and then dissipated—either leaving the light or thinning into the air. Her eyes were wide, unblinking, a frozen gaze, too worn to cry even if she wanted to. Perhaps she had already cried enough that she couldn't do it anymore. She couldn't do anything anymore. Even think clearly. Or rationally.
    There was a couple standing in the park. Abel and Rebecca. She could see them but they didn't notice her on the street bench as far away as she was. They were talking. Then they were hugging. How sweet—someone to keep the other warm on such a laughless lonely evening. She had been following them for a while. She wished she had stopped to eat when they did—her stomach reminded her of that along with the previous meals she had missed.
    Down the street, formless dimensions separated the areas illuminated by overhead lamps. She stood and moved from the light above the bench and into the dark void, tromping down the sidewalk. Something had to happen. Something had to change, she decided, realizing that she might have to be the one to make it change.

Chapter 7

"There's not much I can do for you at this point," the publisher on the other side of the desk said to Abel. "Your catalogue is with a different publishing group."

"Mr. Keene, I don't understand" Abel said. "What does any of this mean?"

"When you started writing songs," Keene said, "you had a catalogue. It's a compilation of all of the songs you've written. You signed with a publisher who owns your entire catalogue. Not only do they own the songs you wrote and signed to them, they own all of the songs you will continue to write as long as you are under that contract."

"Okay, I understand that. But my publisher doesn't want to pitch these songs." Abel was indicating to the CD on the publisher's desk.

"A publisher will pitch anything that will make them money."

"Then why doesn't my publisher want to pitch these?"

"Because they're mostly Christian songs," Keene said. "First of all, with your particular publisher, Christian music is a market that they're not very familiar with. Secondly, there aren't as many Christian stations as there are mainstream radio stations. It's not as large a market. The cost that it would take to put together a presentable demo in order to pitch these songs is not worth the money they think it would bring in. That's considering anyone would pick it up in the first place. Christian music is no less difficult to get into than secular. In fact, it's probably harder."

"But that's who I want to record them. I don't want anyone else to record them. The message will either get lost or they'll butcher it to death."

"I'm sorry," Keene said. "There's not much I can do for you."

"Can't you talk to anyone? Speak to anyone about it? I mean, come on. You know my credibility. If there's a big-name artist with mainstream potential who will record this on an album, don't you think it'll turn my company's head?"

"Yes, I do know your credibility," Keene said, "and it's really not in writing Christian songs."

"But so much is changing," Abel said.

"That's fine. But for the moment, I can't do anything for you."

Abel dug his foot into the carpet, kicking in frustration.

"Don't you have an agent or manager or someone like that who can do this stuff for you?"

He grumbled. "I don't like my agent."

"You did what?" Greg barked. "You went to who?"

"I went to a Christian song publishing firm."

"What for?" Greg asked. "Why would you do that?"

"Because I've been writing a lot of new songs lately."

"Wait a minute...I thought you couldn't play the piano."

"I can't read music. I just couldn't read what was put in front of me. I've been playing the piano for years."

"And so you suddenly decided to write Christian songs?"

"It's what I was inspired to write!" Abel said. "I didn't know I was restricted to only writing secular meaningless pop fluff. You know, I sat down and listened to the radio for ninety minutes one day, and I didn't get a thing out of it."

Greg laughed. "Didn't get a thing out of it? You probably made ninety bucks in the amount of time it took you to find a station."

"That's not why I'm doing this, Greg."

"Listen, don't get all sanctimonious on me. If you want to have your little religion kick, that's fine. But you are what you are and there's nothing you can do about it."

"That's not true, Greg."

"Hey, I know you don't want to face the facts, man. If you want to write Christian songs, that's fine. I don't have any problem with that. Why don't you hand them to me instead of going straight to the publisher? You don't have to do any of that. That's what I'm here for."

"If it's all the same to you, Greg, I'd rather do it myself."

"Hey, no skin off my teeth," Greg said. "Skin off my teeth. Where the heck does that come from? Who has skin on their teeth? Oh well: I'm still getting a cut of what you make anyway."

"Not if I fire you," Abel said intently.

Greg looked at Abel sharply. "What'd you say?"

"What do you do exactly?" Abel asked. "Since I've known you, if I can really say that I know you, you just make sure I have a cell phone and show up to my meetings on time. Well, I have a cell phone, and I'm not going to any meetings or appointments at the moment. So why do I need you?"

Greg smirked. "Are you kidding? What about your bills? Do you pay those? Who do you think takes care of all of that for you?"

"My accountant," Abel said.

"Yeah? Some of those checks your accountant signs goes to me, bucko. Don't think that all I do is sit on my butt and wait for you to start writing again so the dough will come rolling back in."

"Oh, really."

"You can't do this without me!" Greg said. "You don't know what you're doing. You don't even know who you are. You're blind walking around this city, this industry, without me. If someone wants to set up an appointment with you, they don't call you. They call me. I'm the one that saves you from a constant barrage of phone calls so you can win your wife over again and not be bothered with all these petty things. I say yes to some and no to most. Whether you're aware of it or not, I'm working for you daily while you're icing your amnesia. So don't even try to patronize me or you could quickly find yourself out of work."

"If I signed you on to work with me a couple months before my accident, I seriously doubt I wouldn't be able to find work without you."

"Abel," Greg smirked, "babe, this is a cutthroat industry. Even a person who's shown they're worth their salt is expendable. The turnover rate is faster than turnovers at the bakery, man! As soon as your success is over, there's someone else ready to take your place. Do you know how many people want to be you?"

"Greg, I don't care!" Abel said. "I don't care about any of this stuff! Do you want my house? Do you want my car? Then take it! I don't even know how I got it! I don't remember! Fifteen years of my life? Gone. So why couldn't God just take the rest of this crap from me, too, huh? Nothing stopped Him from taking part of my life away. Why should He stop there? And why should He stop with me? Everyone's life I've touched is ruined. I don't want to do this anymore! I want to make a difference in somebody for once. Can't you understand that?"

Before Greg could respond to that, Abel's cell phone rang.

"Why is your cell phone ringing?" Greg said. "I told you to be careful who you gave that number to."

"What?" Abel said, answering his phone, still tense from his and Greg's discussion. "Yes. Really? Uh huh. Okay. Alright, I'll be right down. Thanks. Bye."

"Well who was that?" Greg said.

Abel didn't answer right away, standing there looking at his cell phone.

"What is it?" Greg asked again.

"It was Alex," Abel said.

"Alex? Your lawyer? What'd he want?"

"To tell me that Frank is out of his coma," Abel said. "And he's asking for me."

Abel arrived at the hospital to be greeted by some familiar faces and some not-so-familiar ones. The traffic coming in was kept sparse so not to immediately alert the media. More than likely someone from the hospital was going to do that anyway.

When he walked in the door, members of the Meadows family were there along with some other friends. Trask promptly met Abel upon entering. There also was Rebecca.

After shaking his lawyer's hand, he turned to his wife. "Rebecca? What are you doing here?"

"I was called," she said. "I just thought I should be here for you."

"Thank you so much," he said. "Really. You don't know how much that means."

She reached out for his coat sleeve and laced her fingers up with his. The group of them walked to the elevator and went to the floor where Frank Meadows was being cared for. They were spoken to about his condition on the way up. Frank was paralyzed from the neck down. Various tests were still being done, but the doctors were convinced that his condition was permanent—or at the very least going to require years of physical therapy to recover from.

Rebecca watched Abel's face as these things were being explained to them: about Frank needing help breathing and eating among other things. Abel looked straight ahead at their reflections in the elevator doors with not much of an expression, but it was obviously distressing him, she knew.

The doctors lead them through the halls and to the room where Frank was. Abel saw him through the window before he ever got to the door. He was suspended above the floor, being rotated in a large white apparatus.

Abel was encouraged to go in and see him while Trask and Rebecca remained outside, watching. The room smelled different than the hallway. It was bright with its white walls. A couple of doctors stood in the room, taking readings and observing as the contraption holding Frank Meadows whirred in a quiet hum, turning him forward.

Abel approached slowly as Frank's face came to about eye-level of where he could stand across from him. The moving stopped and there Frank hung at a slight angle to the floor. In his long dark coat, Abel was like the angel of death—a black spot in such a bright room. He certainly felt as out of place.

Frank was looking directly in his eyes, and Abel back at his. He didn't look anything like Abel remembered seeing from his photographs. He was about ten to twelve years Abel's senior. His face looked even older the way he was strung up, so helpless and confined. Yet, in Frank's state, in spite of the situation, he smiled at Abel.

"Hey, kid," Frank said. A chuckle almost accompanied his voice. It was refreshingly happy.

Abel didn't smile back. He couldn't. He partly thought that Frank was delirious. "Hey," he remarked. "How do you…" But he couldn't finish the question. He couldn't find anything to say that deemed remotely appropriate.

"How do I feel?" Frank finished. "Oh, I don't feel much of anything, I'm afraid."

A breath was stuck in Abel's lungs that he couldn't seem to let go of. He had been breathing more shallow since he walked in the room.

"You can say something," Frank said. "It's not like I'm going to punch your lights out."

"Frank," he uttered. "I don't know what to say."

"You don't know too much, do you?" Frank said. "Sorry, bad joke. It's alright. I've been briefed and updated on everybody. I know about your amnesia."

"Yeah," Abel said.

"You want to know something?" Frank said. "If you hadn't showed up, I probably wouldn't have believed you had amnesia."

Abel wasn't quite sure what that meant, but he nodded to him, pursing his lips.

"I'm sorry about Darrel and that other guy."

"David."

"Yeah, David."

"You didn't know him?"

"You didn't either," Frank said. "He was just hanging out with us at the party. Just happened to be at the wrong place at the wrong time."

"You remember all that?" Abel asked.

"Sure," Frank said and chuckled. "You always joked how I had a mind like a steel trap, but you couldn't remember a thing to save your life. Often times I'd tell stories about you to people you couldn't even remember happening." He laughed again. "To tell you the truth, I made some of them up just to mess with you."

Abel smiled finally. "So we were pretty close then?"

"Hey," Frank said, "I've been with you for the past decade, man. There's not a thing we don't know about one another."

"Was I drunk?" he asked.

"Were you drunk? Of course you were drunk. When were you not drunk? That's an exaggeration really, but there wasn't a party you went to where you weren't drunk. We all had too much to drink that night."

Abel felt the corners of his mouth strongly pulling on him, trying to bring his whole body to the ground. His eyes brimmed with tears.

"Frank, I'm so sorry."

"Oh, knock it off," Frank said. "No crying. Look, I'm going to get out of this thing, and we'll be back to kicking butt in no time."

"The doctors aren't giving you very good odds of walking any time soon."

"Doctors," Frank sputtered. "What do they know? Just because they had ten times the schooling we did."

"I dropped out of college."

"Hey, I did too," Frank chuckled. He laughed as though his whole body would shake, but he was completely immobile. His head was strapped in, stationary. He couldn't have even nodded if he wanted to. "Quite a pair we made."

"I'm going to take good care of you," Abel said.

"Dude, I'm loaded," Frank chuckled. "You don't have to do that."
"I'm going to," Abel said. "I want to."
"What's it like?" Frank said.
"What's what like?"
"Losing your memory?" he said. "Having no idea who this guy is strapped up in this piece of crap but knowing you were behind the wheel when it happened anyway?"
"Frank, I…"
"No no no," Frank stammered. "I don't want an apology. You apologized. I want to know what it feels like. I'm serious."
"Confusing," Abel said.
"Come on, you can do better than that. What do you feel? Right now."
"Like I can't breathe."
"Me too," Frank said. "What else? Scared?"
"Yes."
"What else?"
"Lost."
"Pathetic?"
"Yes."
"Like you want to die?"
Abel hesitated. "Yes."
"Good boy," Frank smiled. "Me too. Come on. Get me out of this thing. You can wheel me down to the river and we'll jump in together." He chuckled at that, but Abel couldn't smile. He was choking back tears. "Look at me," Frank said. "This is no more your fault than it is mine. I have no one to hate but myself. We're both idiots. That's about the only way to look at it."
"But if I wasn't driving that car…"
"Then I would have been," Frank said. "It's true. I'm a screw-up too. It happens to the best of us when we let it get the best of us. And you know something?"
"What?"

"There's no hard feelings."

Tears started rolling down Abel's face. He reached out and put his hands around Frank's head, who also started crying.

"Dude, there are people watching."

"Sorry," Abel said and drew back. They both were sniffling and laughing at one another through their tears. Abel motioned to one of the doctors who brought some tissues over to them.

He pulled one out and held it up to Frank's face who promptly blew his nose. "Thanks, mom," he said. They laughed some more as Abel wiped his tears away between the tissue and his thumb.

"You have no idea how much that means to me," Abel said. "This has been so hard. I can't even begin to tell you."

"I want you to," Frank said. "Tell me everything. Things have been changing for you, haven't they?"

Abel nodded.

"Tell me all of it. It's not like I'm going anywhere for a while."

Abel rest his forehead against Frank's.

"Quite the pair we make," Frank said.

Rebecca rest her forehead against the glass, watching.

She looked out the window at the interchanging red lights blinking one then the other, off-rhythm to the sounding bells as the crossing gate came down separating traffic from the tracks running perpendicular to the road. The train whistle sounded in the distance, but Rebecca's thoughts were elsewhere.

"We lived pretty close to railroad tracks," Abel said, looking in the direction the approaching engine-light came from. "I could see the trains go by from my upstairs bedroom window. Every time I heard a train horn, I used to race upstairs to watch it go by. I loved trains. I always had a train set." Then he chuckled. "I always wrecked a train set."

The slow-moving freight came chugging by. Rebecca didn't catch much of what Abel was saying. She came back to attention once the train sounded its horn right in front of them.

"Are you okay over there?" he asked her.
"What?" she said. "Yeah, I'm fine."
"What are you thinking about?"
She only shook her head, her blonde ponytail brushing against the seat behind her.
"Do you want to stop for ice cream?"
She shook her head "no" again.
"Are you sure you're alright?"
"I'm just thinking," she said.
"About what?"
"About Frank."
"Me, too," Abel said. "Did you know him before the accident? Had you ever met him before?"
"A few times," she said. Suddenly her face screwed up and she was covering her expression with her hands, sobbing uncontrollably.
"Rebecca?" Abel put the car in park and let his foot of the break so he could turn toward her. "Rebecca, what is it? What's wrong?" Hunched over, her body shook, her cries heard from her hands over her face. Abel rubbed her back trying to get her to speak to him. "Rebecca?"
She lifted her face, soaked with tears even after only a few seconds. "I just don't know what my problem is."
"You just need to rest," he said. "It's been a long few months."
"No, it's not that," she said, still fighting her cries. "I don't know why this has been so hard for me. And I'm only making it hard on myself—all this bitterness I have toward you. All this bitterness I have toward myself. It's all so ridiculous."
"Sweetie, it's not so ridiculous. I understand."
"No, but I don't understand," she sobbed, collapsing her hands in her lap. "I don't know why it's been so hard to forgive you. I won't even let you apologize to me so I won't feel like I have to forgive you. All you've been wanting is exactly what I've been wanting and that's a chance to start over again. A chance to fall in love again. But I haven't been giving that to you and I don't know why."

"I hurt you," he said.

"But you're not hurting me now," she said. "You're trying to help me and I'm not letting you. You're not the same person I knew before the accident. You're a different Abel than the one I knew."

"I'm sorry. I'm trying."

"No, don't try," she said. "Stop being sorry! I love you more than I ever loved him!"

Abel's heart leapt in his chest. He remained attentive to her.

"Here I am bottling up all this anger toward you and here is this man paralyzed over his whole body, completely helpless, and he could still forgive you and I couldn't."

"Rebecca…"

He reached out to hold her but she only pushed him away saying, "No, not like this." She reached for the door handle and pulled on it. She struck the window with her hand and finally got enough sense of herself to unlock the door before she could get out.

"Rebecca? What are you doing? Rebecca?!"

He got out of his seat and went after her. They met each other at the front of the car. She was only trying to come around to his side of the vehicle. She threw herself at him, her arms around his neck, clutching to him. Stunned for the moment, Abel didn't react right away, but he put his arms around her and held her too. There they stood between the headlights and the crossing gate that separated them from the train continuing to clack on by.

There she clung to him as she sobbed; "I'm sorry. I'm so, so sorry."

"Rebecca, you don't have anything to be sorry for."

Her words were muffled against his shoulder. "Will you please forgive me?"

He cradled her neck in his hands and pulled her away from him. "Of course I forgive you."

"And I you," she said, barely getting out the last word before she pulled his face to her, kissing him longingly, passionately, as though it were the first time and the last in the same embrace, fumbling over each other, trying to hold and express all at once.

She was standing on her tip-toes to reach him, and after a long exchange, slowly began to let herself down as the last of the train trudged by. The drivers behind them started to honk, even before the crossing gates went up. "We'd better go," he said softly to her, "or they'll throw us in front of the next one."

She smiled and kissed him again. "Let's go home."

Chapter 8

"It was incredible," Rebecca said with a dreamy stare into her coffee. "I've never felt those kinds of feelings for him as long as I've known Abel."

"What happened next?" Emily said, craving for her gossip.

Rebecca giggled. "It's not what you think.

"Well?" Emily pushed. "What happened?"

Abel and Rebecca were still kissing one another when they burst through the door. The house was dark, everything silent after the door banged shut again. The couple's arms tightened around one another, pressed against the door, still exchanging affection in hastened kisses.

Rebecca, running her hands up and down her husband's back, broke from his face for a moment to say to him, softly yet insistent: "Please say that you'll sleep with me tonight."

"Tonight?" Abel asked, resting his head against the door behind him. "You want me to sleep with you?"

Rebecca was kissing his face and neck. "I want you to." When Abel didn't say anything more, she began pulling on his hand, leading them toward the hall that extended to the master bedroom.

"Rebecca," he said slowly. They were whispering as though there were someone to wake in the house. "I've never done this before."

"It's okay," she smiled, which he could still see her through what little light was getting in. "I'll take care of you."

"No, no," he said, pulling on her to stop. "You don't understand. I've never done this before. I don't know what I'm doing. I don't know what's happening here. I mean...Rebecca, I don't even remember our wedding. I don't remember making any sort of vows to you. Don't you think that's important? For me to remember that?"

Still holding on to his hand, she took a step forward and rest her forehead against his chin. "You're right," she murmured. "I'm sorry."

He chuckled a bit. "You don't have anything to be sorry for." He leaned back to look at her, cupping her face in his hands. "I'm being given a chance to do this all over again. And I want to do it right."

She nodded, "Me, too," she said, but couldn't prevent that slight inflection of disappointment.

"It's because I love you," Abel said.

"I love you, too."

They kissed once more, Rebecca wrapping her thin fingers around his wrists, his hands cupping her face.

"Now then," Abel smiled, "I'm going to go sleep in the bedroom off the studio." When he stepped out of the hallway, he noticed Rebecca following him. "Where are you going?" he asked.

"To one of the guestrooms," she said. "Did you know that I sleep in the guest room?"

"No, I didn't know that," he said.

She nodded. "I don't sleep in our bed without you. I never have."

"Now that has got to be the absolute sweetest thing I've ever heard," Emily chimed.

Rebecca was all smiles. "We had breakfast together this morning and talked and laughed about anything and everything. We named the birds in the tree outside the window. And dumb things like why our 'yard' isn't a 'yard.' It's multiple 'acres'."

"That's dumb," Emily said.

Rebecca laughed. "I know, but it was so great. We weren't talking about the past anymore—we were just being ourselves. Flirting and commenting on one another. It's like being engaged again."

"And you only have the honeymoon to look forward to."

The both of them laughed. "I've never been in love like this before," Rebecca said. "I mean, even before all of this. This is different."

"It's a new start," Emily said.

"Yeah. I try to look at it that way. But it's like I can't also help but look at the way things were and see how wrong all of it was. This new beginning has also made light of how bad the past really was. You know?"

Emily nodded, thinking for a moment. "Perhaps it is so you can learn from that experience and appreciate the joy that is found in the grace of starting over. Don't dwell on the past. Don't let it take away from how good this is now."

"I know," Rebecca said. "It's just new. And kind of scary, too. But it's all so thrilling I can't even describe it."

The two of them had met together for lunch as they sometimes did at a little outdoor café downtown. There the two wives shared about their husbands and their lives away from the business of it all.

"What is he doing today?" Emily asked.

"He's pitching songs still," she said, which came with a lengthened sigh. "Someone really important was coming in today he was meeting with at a suite in one of the hotels downtown."

"Why the sigh?" Emily asked.

Rebecca smiled. "Because it's work," she said. "And I miss him."

Love from the beginning
Makes our lives worth living

GABRIEL PETER

With breath in heaven's kiss, a reason to exist
When the words are spoken
Many hearts are broken
For such a simple thing
We'd give anything
For what it brings

And I would fall
To be with you
I would fall in love with you

Men of wealth and power
In their final hour
Will look back on their lives and be unsatisfied
Brave and fearsome soldier
Armed from heel to shoulder
Can't keep his tender heart
From being torn apart
He lets down his guard

And I would fall
To be with you
I would fall in love with you

Great celestial being
Finds our lives worth meaning
And leaves his royal throne
For earth to roam
So we won't be alone

And I would fall
To be with you
I would fall in love with you

"That was good," said the gentleman in black. "I like that."

Abel turned himself around where he sat at the piano bench. "You think so?"

"Yeah, very much. It's a love song and yet is still daring enough to throw in some Biblical truth. Interesting approach."

Benjamin Paul wasn't around in the era that Abel West could last remember listening to his radio. His successes as a singer/songwriter were gradually changing the way people listened to music, and the industry was aware of his touch. Having started his own entertainment industry, he among others behind him were in search of the new talents putting substance in their music.

Mr. Keene, the publisher that Abel had previously been talking to, managed to hook up a meeting between he and Benjamin Paul. Knowing of Abel West's talent and acclaim, Benjamin decided to pay him a personal visit. He had a couple companions with him. What their association was with Benjamin wasn't stated, but he would indicate to them occasionally when he addressed himself in the collective "we."

"That particular song," Benjamin analyzed, "would work in a secular and a Christian market. It implies God without being blatant or shoving it down anyone's throat. If you put a drum loop behind it, perhaps, and had someone sing it that usually performs those kinds of mixes, it could do real well."

"Well I don't really know anything about the production aspect of things."

"That's alright, that's alright," Benjamin said. "That wouldn't be up to you anyway. The one you did before that one…"

"Oh, you mean *Darling?*"

"Yeah. That one is a hit song. Undoubtedly. Straight to number one. But I'm sure I don't have to tell you that."

Abel chuckled, sitting on the piano bench with his elbows on his knees. "Well, I don't really know."

"Right, right. My apologies."

Benjamin was very smooth. He didn't have the eccentricity that Abel had encountered with others in pitching his songs. In fact, Benjamin's lesser enthusiasm made him more believable, saying what he thought and not really trying to butter Abel up.

"Wherever your talent is derived from, you obviously have it," Benjamin said. "I notice that a lot of the songs you showed me somehow relate to prayer."

"Yes."

"Very relatable subject. I don't think that'd be a problem at all. You're certainly not as redundant as the number of praise songs that are out there. There's definitely a market for your material."

"You're a secular artist," Abel said. "Weren't you going to help me get these songs to some Christian artists?"

Benjamin smiled. "Handel, Bach, Beethoven, Mozart—all wrote music for kings and for God. The ones without choirs or lyrics, though they didn't speak a Christian word, were still for God. We honor him and minister in Jesus' name in any way we can. Of course," Benjamin said, changing his tone, "there's that pesky matter about the publishing companies."

"I know," Abel said. "I hate it."

"Still, there are ways around it." He winked at Abel and pointed to one of the fellows sitting next to him. "We're going to do some homework. I have your number and I'll definitely be in touch." He reached out to shake Abel's hand. "What did you do," Benjamin said, "writing songs like you did before? You have hundreds of hit songs. Don't take this the wrong way, but many of them don't say a thing."

Abel nodded. "So I've noticed."

"How did that make you feel?"

"I would imagine that I didn't," Abel said with a moderate chuckle. "I didn't feel at all. But I don't remember."

Benjamin smiled. It was infectious. Even his eyes smiled. There was a twinkle that contained a much larger fire.

"You won't have to remember," he said. "Don't worry."

"Two simple sentences, and it was the best advice I've heard in weeks," Abel said, chatting on his phone as he walked through the hotel lobby. "He didn't even mean it that way, but it just spoke something else to me entirely… No, I need to make another stop first, but I'll be sure to call and let you know… Okay. Hey, thank you so much for praying for me. I love you. Talk to you soon."

The sidewalk bellboy held Abel's limo door open for him as the smiling songwriter tipped him and got in. Abel indicated to the driver where to take him. The limo was small, unlike the larger stretch limos, but that's what Abel wanted both in modesty and to not attract so much attention. As many phone calls as he was making and receiving, it was nice to be chauffeured around.

He opened up his notebook and went through a few of his notes from the day's visits. Being mildly distracted by other things, his attention turned toward the window as he watched the city pass by. His eyes turned toward the front of the car catching the limo driver in the rearview mirror. The driver's eyes looked at him and then the road, at him then the road, then down to the left as the opaque shield rolled up between them. It made Abel smirk.

"Strange drivers," he said to himself.

His cell phone rang. "Hello… Hey, yeah, I remember you. I'm glad you called… Yeah, I suppose I've heard of him… No kidding? Well when would that be? Okay, do you have a number for me to call or contact him?" He clicked his pen open and began to write on the paper in front of him. "Uh huh… Uh huh… Okay. Does he have hours I need to call him, or… Okay, I'll do that. Hey, thank you so much. I can't tell you how much I appreciate it. I have another call. Let me let you go… Yeah, bye." He pushed a button. "This is Abel. Hey, Jared, how's it going? Yeah, I did. Some things have come up that I want to talk to you about… No, it's not an emergency, don't worry about it. Just some things I wanted to visit with you about… Okay, we'll do that."

Jared started saying something to him but Abel suddenly lost his role in the conversation when he noticed they weren't going the right direction.

"Hang on a second, Jared." He thumped on the opaque shield. "Hey, driver! Hey, we need to go back the other way!" Into the phone, he said, "Jared, I'm going to have to let you go... Okay. Yeah, we'll do that. Chat with you later."

Abel dropped the phone into the seat and slapped the shield with a flat hand. "Driver! Hey, driver! Turn it around, will you?"

He looked out the window and noticed the cars they were whizzing by, picking up speed, moving significantly faster than the flow of traffic.

"Hey, what is this, a taxi service? Slow it down!"

Horns began honking, cars slamming on their breaks to avoid a broadside collision. The driver was dodging red lights, racing the street on a downhill slope. They hit a place where the ground leveled and the car leaped into the air a few feet before crashing down on its front wheels, resuming its speedy decent.

"Driver!" Abel yelled. "Driver, stop! Stop the car!"

The locks were gone. There was nothing to pull out or switch to get the door to unlatch. He pulled on the handle as hard as he could, kicking at the door, trying to break it open—something. Anything. When that didn't work, he slid over to the other side, trying to force the door by throwing his shoulder into it while pulling on the handle. He laid lengthwise across the seat kicking with all his might at the window trying to break it out.

Where was his cell phone? He looked around for it frantically. Where had it gone? Under the seat? Under his coat?

He looked out the window. The intersections were less controlled, moving into a place with less traffic. Older buildings. Abel knew where they were—the river.

He threw himself down on the floor nearest to the front, pushing his back against it, bracing himself. Next to him was his phone!—on the floor right in front of his face. As he reached out for it, the car went airborne. The wheels roared without the friction of the road beneath them, accelerating rotation as the vehicle dove forward. Abel did his best to keep himself on the floor, his back against the wall, hoping to resist the force of the impact.

The car plunged nose first into the river, submerging most of it from the speed of the impact, then bobbing back to the surface like a cork.

Abel bounced around inside, the wind knocked completely out of him and making his head spin. He managed to keep himself, coughing and wheezing to get air back in his lungs. He was breathing again—hard, fast, panicked. The car was going under. He had to get out.

He put himself in the seat again, struggling to stay there since the car wasn't level, nose down into the water. He kicked at the same window he fought at before. The first blow made the glass cloud over from the impact. A second kick with both feet and the window broke free.

Abel couldn't get himself up fast enough. As soon as he scrambled for the window, the car passed below the waterline and the river started coming in fast. He couldn't fight the intake to get out.

"Jesus, please get me out of this," he cried.

He breathed in several times, readying himself to swim for it, and finally took one last breath just as the water completely overcame the backseat. With as much strength as he could muster, he put both hands on either side of the window, what glass was left cutting into his palms, and slingshot himself out, kicking and flailing toward the surface.

When his head broke, he choked and gagged, rolling his head backwards and attempting to float, but his body was still shaking too much. His hands clawed at the surface of the water as though there was something to grasp. Sure enough, something came within his reach floating under his arm before he even knew it was there. He scrambled for it, and looked up in the direction where the vehicle had just come from.

There they were—several police cars at the scene of his rescue.

Abel sat on the back of the ambulance with a blanket draped over his shoulders. Various emergency crew stood about him while his brother, Jared, stood just off to the side. About an hour and a half had passed since the accident and the light of the afternoon was dimming. Abel was still damp and had been urged to go to the hospital, but he didn't want to just yet, if he would at all.

One of the detectives came around the side of the ambulance just behind Jared. "Our divers are up," the detective said.

"What'd they find?" Jared asked.

The officer handed Abel a plastic bag full of Abel's things—including a ruined cell phone. "They found no one."

"No one?" Abel said in surprise. "No driver? Nothing?"

"Only this in the front seat." The detective held out a metal pipe.

"I don't understand," Abel said.

"This was wedged between the seat and the gas pedal," the detective said. "It's possible that he jettisoned long before the car started picking up speed. You didn't see anyone?"

"No, I didn't," Abel said. "I told you—I made eye contact with him and that was it. He rolled the shield up and that's all I…"

"Did you get a good look at the driver?"

Abel shrugged. "I guess. I don't know."

"Any particular race?"

"He seemed to be Caucasian," Abel said.

"And you're sure it was a man."

Abel thought about it. "I guess so."

"You have to be sure, Mr. West," the detective said. "Was it a man or a woman?"

He shook his head. "I can't say for sure."

"We're still waiting for witness accounts: see if anyone saw anything like a driver escaping a moving vehicle. From what we know so far, I don't think the intention was ever to drop you in the river. I think the driver was just trying to cause an accident. If that's really the truth, you drove quite a ways before you got to the river. It's pretty remarkable the car stayed under control for that long."

"You must have some army of guardian angels watching out for you," Jared said.

"I'm beginning to feel that way," Abel said.

"One of our guys talked to one of the bellhops over at the hotel," the detective continued, "and he said he remembered putting you in the car but couldn't recall specifically looking at the driver."

"It's just one of those things I don't think about," Abel said.

"Yeah, we know," said the detective. "Can you name anyone that could possibly want to kill you?"

"He was asked all that already," Jared said.

"I told them I didn't know," Abel added. "I can't think of anyone who would want to kill me, really."

The detective stuck his pen back into his jacket. "Well, since you can't remember the limo service you called, we're still waiting for something else. The tags don't register. We're looking into the families that were related to the victims of that car accident you were in."

"Really?" Abel said. "You think one of them might want to kill me?"

"It's a possibility," the detective said. "There might be something significant in wanting to make it look like you were killed in a car wreck."

"Just be careful," Abel said. "Really. I've already caused them too much grief. They don't need anymore."

"We'll do our best." The detective looked toward an officer that was patiently waiting to interrupt. "What's up?"

"There's a woman here," the officer said to the detective and then to Abel, "Says she's your wife."

"My wife?" Abel said.

Apparently Rebecca managed to get through security before Abel could tell the officer to let her through. She was pushing around the corner and straight into his arms, clinging to him and shaking as though she had just been in the river herself. They kissed and held one another, rocking back and forth, murmuring sweet appreciations and thanksgivings.

"Well would you look at that," Jared said with a chuckle. "Gosh, I never thought I'd see the sight."

"Hi, Jared," Rebecca said to him, feeling a little embarrassed.

"Hey, Rebecca. So what is this? When did all of this happen?"

"It's still happening," Abel said. "It's just taking a little time."

"Well congratulations," Jared said.

"And you're invited to the wedding, of course," Rebecca said.

"Wedding?" Jared asked. "What wedding? You mean the two of you? Hasn't that already happened once?"

Chapter 9

Most of the earliest memories of Abel's new life came from this office. He didn't think he would find himself sitting in it again. A business card holder had a swiveling pen attached to it that Abel was spinning around in his fingers, next to the nameplate that read "Alexander Trask: Attorney at Law."

"Sorry to keep you waiting," Trask said, coming into the office through the door behind Abel. "Some meetings take longer than I expect."

"It's quite alright," Abel said.

Trask sat down at his desk. "What can I do for you?"

"I came to give you this," Abel said, handing him an envelope. "I know I could have given it to your secretary, but I wanted to hand it to you in person."

"Thank you," Trask said, looking at the envelope. "What is it?"

"It's an invitation."

"An invitation to what?"

"To Rebecca and I's wedding. We're renewing our wedding vows and we would like for you to attend."

"Thank you very much," Trask said. "That's very kind of you." He tapped the envelope a few times in his hand.

"Is there something wrong?" Abel asked.

"Oh," Trask sighed, "I don't know."

"Is this about your wife?"

Trask stopped fidgeting and looked at him intently. "What about my wife?"

"Specifically," Abel began timidly, "me and your wife."

"You know about that?"

"Yes. Rebecca told me."

"Nothing was ever proven."

"She told me that, too," Abel said. "Why did you represent me in court if I did that to you?"

"Oh," Trask sighed again, "I suppose it was for selfish reasons. I didn't want my wife and my home life plastered all over the news in such personal detail as yours was."

"I'm sorry," Abel said.

"You didn't know," Trask replied. "And that's what made it at least somewhat bearable."

"I've been getting the 'you didn't know' response a lot, actually," Abel said.

"It's okay," Trask added. "It's over."

"I was thinking about speaking to your wife," Abel said. "I didn't want to do that without your permission first."

"You couldn't if you wanted to," Trask said. "I haven't seen her in a few days."

"Really?"

"She does this occasionally. It's her thing. It's the way she deals with stress. Sometimes she goes up to our cabin. She might be there. I don't know."

There was a bit of silence between them.

"Listen," Trask said, "I understand that you have good intentions. It's admirable, really. But I don't think you should talk to her. I don't think it would solve anything—especially for her. We're all responsible for our own actions. You and Rebecca deal with yours and we'll deal with ours."

"Okay," Abel complied.

"Be careful digging up all this past," Trask said. "I know you're just trying to get a handle on things, but it's not only your past you're messing with."

"That's good advice," Abel said.

"That's what I'm here for," Trask said, standing. Abel stood with him. "Abel," Trask added, "if it's all the same to you," he handed the envelope back to his client; "I think we should just keep this relationship professional."

Abel looked at the envelope for a moment and finally reached out to take it from him. When he pulled it from his fingers, Trask's hand remained extended to him, open. "No hard feelings," Trask said.

Abel shook his hand. "No hard feelings."

"Congratulations to you both."

"I hope this one will be happier than the first one," Frank said, laughing.

"We're doing fine," Abel said, walking pace with Frank's electric wheelchair as they traveled the hospital grounds so his friend could get some sun. "You're going to be invited to the wedding, of course."

"Talk about déjà vu," Frank said. They both laughed. "I don't know that I'll be up and on my feet by then to be a groomsman for you again."

"It's still a month away," Abel said. "We're still planning and taking the time to know one another again."

"What if you find something you don't like about each other?" Frank said. "It's not like you can call off the engagement."

"No, this is for us," he said. "We're already committed to being together. We just want to make it real. You know—considering that I don't remember the first one."

"Right," Frank said. "Think they'll ever find your killer? Or rather—the person that tried to kill you?"

"I have no idea," Abel replied. "I don't know who would possibly want to kill me. There's no telling what kinds of enemies I made before I can remember."

"How much memory of yours did you lose anyway?"

"About fifteen years."

"What's the last thing that you remember? I mean the very last thing," Frank said. "What is the last possible event you can recall before waking up from your car accident?"

Abel thought about it a moment and shrugged. "I really have no idea. I've never really thought about it that specifically."

"I want you to try," Dr. Corin said to him. "Think of the very last thing when you were nineteen years old that you can remember before the accident."

Rebecca's fingers were laced into Abel's hand, her other resting lightly on his arm, there for her husband with whatever support that he needed. Dr. Corin requested that she be there, and Abel wanted her to be. Abel's knee was bouncing a little bit, his eyes looking down and away, trying to recall as best as he could. "I can remember a party," Abel said. "I remember not wanting to be there."

"Where was this party?" Dr. Corin asked.

Abel's head pivoted slowly back and forth as he tried to remember. "A dorm room maybe?"

"Do you remember dropping out of college, Abel?"

"I don't know," Abel said.

"Are you sure?" the doctor asked. "Think hard. Why did you drop out of college?"

Abel sat neither thinking about it nor trying to recall. "I don't remember dropping out of college."

"Think harder," Corin urged. "Think of home. Think of things that were happening at home."

"My dad," Abel said.

"Your dad killed himself."

"Yeah."

"How did you feel about that?"

"I was mad," Abel said. "I was mad at him for abandoning us. He gambled himself into debt and felt like he was doing us a better service by leaving us. Abandoning mom and April. And then just giving up completely. I said I didn't care, but that wasn't true." Abel slowly took his next breath and released it in a sigh. "And I think in some way I was also mad at Jared for not wanting to help out. But he already had his family he was having to care for. Emily was expecting their first."

"You remember Emily being pregnant?" Corin asked.

"Yes. In fact, she may have even had the baby. We didn't keep in touch that well."

"Do you remember your sister having the baby?" Corin asked.

He didn't answer. His sister, April, was pregnant. He could remember that.

"Abel," Dr. Corin asked. "Do you remember her having the baby?"

"No," he said.

Corin looked at him, intently. "Yes, you do."

"I'm here to see April West." Abel could see the woman behind the counter. He could remember the inside of the emergency room. He could see sad faces. There were tears.

"When did she get pregnant?" Dr. Corin asked.

"While she was in high school," Abel said. "I remember being so upset about that. I remember thinking I wanted to kill the guy that did that to her. I think I ignored that my sister was sleeping around." His eyes trailed off, looking into some random part of the room. "I don't remember dropping out of college."

He picked up the phone. "Abel, this is mom. We're taking April to the emergency room. We don't want you to worry and we don't expect you to be there. We think she's going into labor."

"I wanted to go home," Abel said.

"Wanted to go home from where?" Dr. Corin asked. "From school? When did you go home?"

"To see my sister."

"Why did you go home to see your sister?"

Abel shook his head slightly. "Something was wrong." He was beginning to remember.

Abel looked at the empty bed. This is where they said she would be. She should have been in this room. Everything looked suddenly abandoned. There was blood on the sheets and some on the floor. All was in disarray. Something went wrong.

"I'm sorry, excuse me, sir?" Someone in white got Abel's attention. "You can't be here. I'm going to have to ask you to go downstairs."

"What happened in here?" Abel said.

"You need to go back downstairs."

"My sister is supposed to be in here."

"There hasn't been anyone in this room for a while," said the orderly.

"They told me downstairs to come up here."

"Then you need to check in at the desk first."

Abel walked back down the hall to the desk and tried to get the attention of the woman on the phone. When she didn't seem to notice him nor wanted to stop talking, he cut in.

"Excuse me," he said. "I'm sorry. I've been waiting for a while. Could you tell me what room April West is in please?"

The nurse pinched the phone between her cheek and shoulder as she fingered through a set of files. She pulled one out and opened it. "Your sister is in room two-eighteen."

"Yes, I was just over there," Abel said.

"Then I don't know. You'll just have to go downstairs."

"They said downstairs to come up here."

The nurse made a face and some sort of exasperated sigh as she flipped through another set of folders. "Hi, Ginny," she said into the phone. "Can you hang on just a second for me?" She set the phone down and found the file she was looking for. "April West has been moved up to OR," the nurse said.

"Where is that?" Abel asked.

"You can't go up there."

"Is there another desk upstairs?"

"Excuse me a moment," the nurse said, picking the phone up again. "Hey, Ginny? Are you still there? Sorry to keep you waiting..."

Abel walked to the stairs at the end of the hall. He went up one floor, opened the door, and asked if this was the floor for the operating room. Someone told him it was the next one up, so he marched another flight of stairs and to another hallway.

This floor felt rather vacant. The lights seemed to be dimmer, or there were fewer of them. He could see a pair of surgeons through the window of the door in front of him, washing their hands, blood on their clothes. Continuing up the hallway, Abel walked to the pair of double doors at the end. There on the operating table was his sister.

Abel's eyes were wide. Dry. His ears rang. He walked from one quiet space to an even quieter room as he pushed through the swinging door. There was blood all over her, blood on the floor. She lay there with a tube in her mouth, the equipment next to her still alive. But she was not. There were no beeps to indicate her pulse, no hiss sounding her breathing. She was still.

He walked up to the bed and looked down at her, gaping in disbelief. He reached out his hand very carefully and very slowly touched her head. Tears began to brim on the edge of his eyes. But he still couldn't blink. He couldn't feel anything.

"I'm sorry, Abel," came a voice behind him.

He turned and saw Jared walking in through the doors.

"I tried to get you downstairs before you came up. I must have just missed you."

Abel looked back at his sister. "What happened?" he asked.

"Complications during labor," he said.

"During labor?" Abel asked. "I thought she wasn't due for a few more weeks."

"This one wanted to come early," Jared said.

"Where's mom?" Abel asked.

"She's downstairs."

"My baby sister," Abel murmured.

Jared let him look at her for a while before he reached out and tugged on his brother's shoulder. "Come on," he said. "Let's go downstairs." They stepped through the double doors before Abel rolled away from Jared's arm.

"No," Abel said. "I want to see her."

"She's gone, Abel."

"Gone? Well, where have you been?" Abel barked. "Why haven't you been here?"

"What do you mean?" Jared asked. "Abel, I have a job, I have a family of my own."

"I knew I shouldn't have stayed at school. You told me you were going to take care of this."

"Yeah, I was sending them money," Jared said. "You needed to stay in school. Get your education. That way you can..."

"No. No, you should have been here. I should have been here."

"Abel, you're just upset."

"Of course I'm upset!" Abel shouted. "My sister is dead! She's dead, Jared! Do you see?"

"Abel, I was there," Jared said. "I was here when it happened. There's nothing that could have been done."

"There's nothing that could have been done?" Abel jeered. "How about if dad stayed put? Maybe April wouldn't have become such a tramp. And how about if mom..."

"Hey, you watch it," Jared said. "This is nobody's fault. Blame is just your opinion. We can't possibly understand what God would have intended in something like..."

"Don't you talk to me about God's plan," Abel interrupted. "Don't you ever say that to me again. That's such lame Christian verbiage, some tell-all answer that explains all tragedy as being unexplainable. Is that supposed to make me want to run to God and jump right into His arms? He's there no matter what. Isn't that what you want to tell me? When we are happy and things are just hunky-dorey, it's easy to believe in God. There's almost no sense in needing God. We would even say it's imposing of God to come into our lives when times are good. But when things start to really bottom out, we are groveling in a pit of despair, when we need God to be there to pull us out, what do we find? Nothing. There's no God pulling me out of this. Why is he so present when times are good and so absent in times of trouble? All my life growing up in church I heard God described as the Father. Our earthly fathers are supposed to be a living example of what God is to His children, right? Well our father left us, Jared. Our father abandoned us. And before that, he was withdrawn, he was moody, and not very nice or encouraging to any of us. So if that is all I know of a father to be, how am I supposed to understand that God is the infallible, omnipresent, loving resource to all our pain? Huh? How? Especially when our father is the cause of most of our pain."

"Please be careful, Abel," Jared said. "You are on the verge of something dangerous if you are ready to convince yourself of these things."

"No, no," Abel said, almost laughing. "No, I believe in God. But maybe I'm starting to see what He's really like—just the cosmic sadist that He is. If April is now safe in God's hands, why was she not safe in His hands before? God's goodness is so inconsistent here in this life—hurting us and watching us suffer. So why should heaven be any different? Isn't there also a hell? Why would He not hurt us after death just as He would before it?"

"Listen," Jared said, holding up his hand, gesturing for Abel to calm down, "I'm not going to say I know how you feel right now. And I'm not going to try and talk you down. At the very least—the kindest thing you can do, Abel—is put on a good face for mom. How hard do you think all of this has been for her?"

"I'd rather be pissed off," Abel said. "At least my anger is honest. She's as selfish as dad was, Jared. First our dad, now our sister—who's going to be next? And how much of it could have not happened because of the idiocy of another? If my mother won't accept me in my anger, will she also reject me in my joy or in my pain? No, I'm not going to pretend to change my attitude so that another person can have theirs."

Jared's eyes trailed down, his gaze somewhere in the vicinity of Abel's pockets. His lips were pursed, his arms crossed.

"Then perhaps you should leave," he said to Abel, without looking up at him.

Abel made a face like he had just been slapped. The screwed expression that sharpened his features during his ranting now became one of shock and confusion.

"So," Abel started. "I'm not welcome here either."

"This is not the time to pick your battles," Jared said solemnly. "I just think it's better if you go somewhere to cool off."

Abel jutted his chin out, both thinking and biting his tongue. "Yeah," he said. Not finding another word, he turned and started down the hall.

"Where are you going?" Jared asked.

"Away," Abel said.

"And that was the last any of your family saw of you for a long time," Dr. Corin said. "Do you remember anything else that happened after that?"

Abel slowly shook his head.

Dr. Corin hummed his suspicions and nodded. "You probably never will. I imagine this particular incident is where your memory cuts off. This is what you were repressing. It was your transformation from the Abel of your past to the Abel of your future. After you left the hospital that night, you went back to school. The next evening, you got drunk with a bunch of your college pals and you got into a car accident. You weren't driving. But you were the only one to survive."

Abel reached up and touched the scar just beyond his hairline. "Is everyone alright," he muttered.

"I beg your pardon?" Dr. Corin asked.

"Nothing," Abel said. "I can kind of remember that. Vaguely. It's like there are two memories of two different events merging together."

"When you were recovered from the accident," Dr. Corin continued, "you gave the hospital no next of kin. You said there was no one to contact, and that's the way they have you down in the record. After you were better, you went to jail for a short time being involved with a drunk-driving accident and drinking underage. What happened after that is anyone's guess."

"I started writing songs for Priority Mail," Abel said; "a rock band looking for a lead singer. I couldn't sing like they wanted, but I could write."

"Do you remember that?" Dr. Corin asked.

Abel shook his head. "I read about it." His wife squeezed his hand. He turned his head her direction and half-smiled, but wasn't making eye-contact. "So many regrets," he said. "I should have been there when my mom died. I was just so angry. I had lost my dad, my sister, my sister's baby…"

"Not necessarily," Dr. Corin said.

"What do you mean?" Abel asked. Rebecca looked at the doctor, too.

"Your sister had a son," Dr. Corin said. "You weren't around long enough to know he'd survived the incident."

"Her son?" Abel said. "Where is he? Do you know where he is?"

Dr. Corin hesitated. "I don't know that I'm permitted to say."

Abel rose from his chair. "Doctor, please. Where is my sister's son?"

Dr. Corin looked into Abel's face.

"Ask your brother."

"We adopted him," Jared said.

Abel and Jared were sitting on a park bench on a pleasantly beautiful weekend watching the children play. The sun was shining directly into their faces, so the children only appeared as shadows, leaping and running, swinging, throwing things at one another, and laughing. They were angels in the daylight seen only through the faintest of visions.

"Mom had taken him first," Jared said. "She and Emily both nurtured him through his infancy. Around the time he learned to walk, mom was diagnosed with cancer. I was the next of kin and the child had no other legal guardian. The father of the boy was still a minor and didn't want to have anything to do with him anyway."

Jared's oldest wasn't roughing with the other children, but she watched them. She was sitting off to the side writing in a notebook.

"She was just a few months older," Jared said of her. "My wife and I knew it was going to be a lot of work, but we wanted to do it." He paused. "Especially since I couldn't be there to care for April when she got pregnant. I probably did it out of guilt, but I love him as though he were my own."

"Why didn't you tell me?" Abel asked.

"You've never known," Jared said looking at him. "You didn't want to know. This is the first time this has ever come out to you. You've been so angry. You should have seen your face. You were going on about how could God was unfair. You disappeared and I didn't see you for years. You didn't appreciate that I was just kind of throwing myself back into your life—that I was imposing, you said."

"How did you find me?" Abel asked.

"It was kind of on accident," Jared said. "I had just moved my business here and was watching this where-are-they-now kind of show on TV. One of the bands they talked about was the band Priority Mail and you were one of the people interviewed. I couldn't believe it. I looked up your name and started reading about all these songs of yours I'd heard and didn't even realize you'd written them. When I decided to try and contact you, I discovered that you were living right here. Otherwise, I mean, I don't keep up with artists and songs or read the liner notes or anything like that. I didn't even know you were really into writing music—which is my own fault, I guess. Our family was always stretched so thin after mom and dad separated."

"I know," Abel said.

"I tried to contact you by passing you messages. I wasn't brave enough to try and call. I finally managed to get a hold of you through an acquaintance. You seemed kind of indifferent about the reunion—almost like you were only meeting with me to be polite. However, you wouldn't tell me at all about where you'd been, and didn't really want to. Eventually, you met the kids and I met your wife. Emily and I invited you to church, but you wouldn't go. You said you had put that life behind you. Your wife, however, became interested. We really learned the most about your life and where you had been the past few years through her. She started going to church with us. Then you became distant again. We prayed for you all the time. We prayed that you would come around and seek God's face again. I sometimes feel like the accident, the one that took away your memory, was my fault, and the death of those people was the cost of it. All because I was praying for something, anything to happen."

"Jared, that wasn't your fault," Abel said. "That was mine."

Jared nodded. "When your memory was gone, and all of these Christian habits started coming back for you after the accident, I just couldn't believe it. It was an answer to prayer. I didn't want to possibly start anything that would send you going back the other direction. I didn't even want to tell you everything that happened after April died. I thought it might bring those memories back."

"Yeah," Abel said.

"You know, Abel, it wasn't easy for me either," Jared said. "None of it was. I was the one that found dad after his suicide. And you know, he tried to make it look like an accident. He was trying to take care of his debts and give money to his kids. But the insurance company later proved it was fraud and his death was a suicide. I tried to keep my distance from him when I was living with him, and then I blamed myself for it after he killed himself thinking if I hadn't been so far away that maybe he wouldn't have done that. I think dad probably thought that waiting until I was married and you were in college to kill himself was his idea of compassion."

"Yeah," Abel murmured again.

"But I mean that whole thing didn't even compare to mom's last few months. They came in what was probably the hardest year of my life. None of it was easy for me. I could have easily gone in the same direction that you did. I could have become depressed and resentful. I could have over-analyzed everything never getting close to anyone because of all the pain I seemed pre-ordained to endure. Like you said to me, God allows us to go through all this hurt, when aren't we supposed to feel safe in his hands? Fortunately, I met this great girl in college that meant the world to me. She was strong when I couldn't be. She introduced me to people, circles of Christians, that really helped to build me up. Yes, there were people who called themselves Christians who seemed like they did everything un-Christian, but I can't blame Jesus on account of how someone else is acting. I had to learn to trust Him. And I found it in the counsel of others. You, on the other hand, didn't have that kind of support system. You didn't want it. You wanted to be alone. You ran away from everyone. We cannot fight these battles of ours on our own. It's too hard. Furthermore, we were never meant to."

"I wish I could remember," Abel said.

"I'm glad you don't," Jared said. "You don't have to remember. Don't worry about the past. Don't think about it. Live for today. You can't even live for yesterday—it's gone. Let it be gone. For some, that's easier than others. For you, God completely wiped the slate clean. It's over. God doesn't remember what you did. The Bible says in Isaiah that he has blotted out your transgressions. He's blotted them out. Then He calls for us to return to Him, and He will make us new."

"But I'm so surrounded by everything old," Abel said. "This world that I created: how do I let that go?"

"That was a different Abel West," Jared said. "Your first songs were so dark. It was the pop songs, the love songs, that made you so popular, earning you your reputation. But it was the rock songs—the dark, brooding lyrics full of hate and spite and everything resentful that showed me what my brother had become. Some of the most popular dark bands out there are as big as they are because of your songs."

"I'm trying to change that," Abel said.

"I'm glad," Jared said. "But don't let yourself go back to that. Don't put yourself back into it to feel like that's how you change it. All of this has happened for a reason. I really truly believe that given this second chance, you're going to change a lot of people, starting with yourself. Songs like that came about because you dwelled on it. Don't dwell on it anymore. It's over. It's gone. I forgive you and so does Rebecca. Let that be it."

"I'm learning that now," Abel said. He watched the children play, his eyes especially on the one that wouldn't ever know his true mother. "I just don't understand why God does the things that He does in the way that He does them."

"I don't either," Jared said, "but we weren't meant to. The Bible says, 'As the heavens are higher than the earth, so are my thoughts higher than your thoughts and my ways are higher than your ways.' We weren't meant to know why God does the things He does. We're just supposed to trust that He knows what He's doing. Jeremiah twenty-nine verse eleven reads, 'For I know the plans I have for you; plans to prosper and not to harm you, to give you a future and a hope.' That's good insight into God's character."

Jared noticed a tear running down Abel's face.

"The forgiveness is there if you want it," Jared said. "God has guaranteed that He is going to give it to you. But you have to take it. In order to truly be forgiven, you can't just believe that God has forgiven you. You have to forgive yourself. In Titus chapter three, there's a verse that says at one time we were all foolish and disobedient and deceived. We lived in malice, it says, hating and being hated. Can you related to that?"

Abel nodded.

"But when the kindness and love of God our Savior appeared," Jared continued, "He saved us, not because of righteous things we had done, but because of His mercy. He saved us not because we were good, but because He wanted to."

"How do you know all these verses and stuff?" Abel said.

"I'm a brother. It's my job."

Abel kind of smirked at that. Jared tussled his hand in Abel's hair.

"Blame is just an opinion," Jared said. "Guilt is just a feeling. Forgiveness—that's something real. That's something to take hold of. That's something to build a life on."

He put his arm around his brother's shoulder and sat there with him, watching angels play in the cool of the day.

Chapter 10

The weeks spent planning their second wedding were some of the happiest that Abel and Rebecca had known, and there was so much more to look forward to. The two of them were so busy apart from one another that it didn't even feel like they lived in the same house together, let alone the same neighborhood. Things were going well with Abel's efforts to get his new songs recorded. In the deal that was pending with Benjamin Paul, Abel was keeping track of his songs as they were laid down into top-notch demo productions to be put in a flashier, more presentable package. The whole process seemed new to Abel. He had been in a studio before, he knew, but not that he could remember.

Benjamin Paul's entertainment company was nearby the offices of many other recording companies and publishers. Abel was making frequent visits to observe production and pitch more songs. After a while, he and Rebecca agreed that he would live in and out of hotels for the month prior to the wedding. They still saw each other when Abel was back in town, and made time to go on dates. The two missed each other terribly, but this way made it feel like a true engagement leading up to the wedding day.

The congregation that gathered to watch them exchange vows was larger than the number of guests they invited the first time around. The majority of them were members of their respected churches in addition to their own friends and sides of the family. The pastor that joined them was Rebecca's own from the church she had been attending with Jared and Emily.

"Dearly beloved," the pastor said in his fatherly resonance. "We have gathered here today to witness to reuniting of these two lovers,

Abel and Rebecca West. These two have decided, before us and before God, to renew their wedding vows in that so precious spiritual bond between a man and a woman, as given to us by God. Their story of renewal should be a testimony to us all that we may strive to be one with our Creator, the very author of love."

The majority of the ceremony had passed. All the while Abel and Rebecca couldn't keep their eyes off one another, smiling so brightly that it would almost burst into rays. Everything happened around them and they just let it pass, lost in a trance with each other.

"Abel," the pastor said to him.

And finally he came into what was happening. "Yes?" he answered.

"Do you take this woman to be your lawfully wedded wife? To…"

"I do," Abel said.

"Now hold on," the pastor said. The congregation laughed. "I haven't finished yet." He waited for the laughter to subside and Abel's embarrassment and nervousness to cool before he began again. "Do you take this woman to be your lawfully wedded wife? To love and to cherish, in sickness and in health, joined together by the Holy Spirit, for as long as you both shall live?"

Abel chuckled and finally said, "I do."

"And Rebecca," the pastor turned to her. "Do you take this man to be your lawfully wedded husband? To love and to cherish, in sickness and in health, joined together by the Holy Spirit, for as long as you both shall live?"

"I do," she said.

"Deuteronomy 4:9," the pastor said, "tells us, 'Do not forget the things your eyes have seen or let them slip from your heart as long as you shall live. Teach them to your children and to their children after them.' What God has joined together, let no man put asunder. I now pronounce you—again—husband and wife. You may kiss your bride."

Abel cupped her face in his hands and kissed her lovingly. Applause erupted around them along with a few more words the pastor spoke, but the couple didn't hear any more of it, lost in each other's embrace.

The reception was grand—a full dinner complete with music and dancing. Abel had hired a live orchestra for the event. He wore a small head mic so that he could dance with his wife to the light jazz playing beneath them and sing to her all the while:

Darling
Wrap me in your arms tonight
Only you can hold me right
Stay with me and hold me tight
There's too much space in the middle
Hey diddle diddle
Would you spend more than a little
Time with me?

Gentle wind
I'm talking to myself again
Just hoping that you'll hear my prayer
Take it where
Someone's listening
Starry skies
I'm looking into heaven's eyes
Don't want to be alone tonight
Shine your light
Into the darkest part of me
I've been here before
Can't do this on my own anymore
Because my tears will fall
After all
I can't hold me

Darling
Wrap me in your arms tonight
Only you can hold me right
Stay with me and hold me tight
There's too much space in the middle
Hey diddle diddle
Would you spend more than a little
Time with me

Both struggled to keep their composure during the song. They swayed back and forth beneath the dim lights before the friends and family that witnessed them here. Occasionally, Abel was kissing his wife's forehead. She would lean into him and just swayed to the music. When it was over, he pulled the microphone off his head and kissed her, the audience applauding with their appreciation and their blessings.

Everyone else joined in the festivities, eating and dancing, visiting and cutting up. The married couple was sitting at their table. Rebecca was telling stories about certain people Abel didn't recognize. They laughed at Frank Meadows spinning circles in his wheelchair. The couple would exchange glances and kiss, truly behaving like newlyweds.

As Abel was whispering into his lady's ear, he felt the presence of someone standing in front of him. He turned to look and saw that man adorned in black standing before them—Benjamin Paul.

"Ben," Abel said, standing up to shake his hand. "I'm glad you could make it! I didn't even know you were here. I didn't see you before the service."

"It was nice," Benjamin said. "I just came to tell you I had to go."

"Well thanks for coming," Abel said.

"I liked your song. You should let someone else hear that."

"Thank you. I have actually."

"I also wanted to give you your wedding present." He pulled something from his coat and handed it to Abel. "Congratulations to you both." He winked at Rebecca as he walked away.

Abel sat down again looking at the rolled up piece of paper in his hands. It was rather old fashioned, held by a red ribbon sealed with wax and the letter "T" strangely pressed into it.

"Do you have any idea what it is?" Rebecca asked him.

"I'm not sure." He broke the seal and managed to slip the ribbon off the paper unrolling it. He skimmed the document briefly. His eyes widened. He looked up to see if he could still catch a glance of Benjamin Paul, but he couldn't be seen.

"What?" Rebecca said. "What is it?"

"It's a contract," Abel said.

"A contract to what?"

"Benjamin Paul bought my catalogue." Then he laughed. "He bought the whole thing! He just bought my whole catalogue."

"What does that mean?"

"What it means to me," Abel smiled, "is that I'm out of my contract. My songs are going to be recorded again."

There was another guest at the wedding—a guest that Abel and Rebecca did not see. She was there to see them exchange vows, and then she wandered away. She rode the bus around the city for a while—a vagabond in her own way, rejecting the warmth of home, the stillness of settling down. The ache of her heart twisted her mind, spilling such contempt into her soul, drowning in it, so unsettled by it that she couldn't get her bearings enough to find a way out. She had become consumed by her own self-loathing.

She hugged herself in her jacket. It wasn't a cold night, but her body felt differently about it. Wedged in the seat against the window, she watched as the world passed by. She wanted so much to be a part of it again. Or maybe she wanted to be a part of a different world. Neither could be had, she knew. They were hopeless dreams. Wanting needlessly, but needing to be wanted.

He didn't want her. He wanted someone else. He was finally with his someone—forever. Such a mistake. It should have never happened in the first place. How could anyone want her ever again? Joy was so far from her it was as though it would never come back. What good was joy to anyone? Just another fleeting temporary emotion as fickle as the changing weather. She was tossed by these storms, the guilt on her conscience. He, on the other hand, was safe in the harbor, with a new wife and a new start. His mind was erased and he could just start all over again. Why wasn't he tossing with her too? He was tossed out to sea with her. They swam here together. Shouldn't he be enduring these raging seas in the same water as she? Shouldn't he also know how it felt?

She was inside now, looking at herself in the mirror, a face that disgusted her so. It made her sick to look at it. Indeed, sometimes she did make herself sick. Sometimes she felt so unlovely, frustrated with herself and her appearance, that she would make herself sick. She hated to eat. She hated anything that sustained her life.

Not anymore. Tonight, it was going to change. This evening, she was going to make it change. Without her, unaware of her, the rest of the world passed by. She didn't want to be in it anymore. But the world would notice her one last time. She would make sure of that. The ones that had forgotten her would remember her always.

Her body shook with delight though her face showed none. She stood there, naked, hating herself. Such a world with such people—with such credulity and disregard. How she hated to see herself. How she hated to see herself in it. She picked up the scissors off the sink. With her other hand, she extended her hair from her head. She began to cut.

Abel and Rebecca kissed in the back of their stretch limousine as the collection of witnesses to their matrimonial celebration ran behind them waving and shouting. Their honeymoon flight wouldn't leave until the next morning. Tonight, they were going to spend time home, alone, together. For the first time that Abel knew, they were going to share the same bed.

He carried his wife into the master bedroom and set her on her feet. She wrapped her arms around his neck and kissed him. The two warmed in this embrace for some time before Rebecca broke to begin unbuttoning his white shirt. Abel rested his forehead against hers and rubbed her hands in his as she fumbled with the buttons.

After a moment, she giggled. "Your hands are shaking."

He smiled. "I'm sorry."

"There's no need to be sorry," she said, kissing him once more.

"I'm afraid I'm a little nervous," he said. "I know I've done this. I just don't remem…"

"Shh," she sounded, placing her finger over his mouth. Replacing her finger with her lips, she kissed him. They began to sway as though they were dancing again.

Rebecca began to whisper to him: "Let him kiss me with the kisses of his mouth, for your love is more delightful than wine. Pleasing is the fragrance of your perfumes; your name is like perfume poured out. Take me away with you. Let us hurry."

She then took him to bed and wrapped him in love.

The two of them lay there on their sides, blankets encircling them, facing one another. They both watched each other's hands as a family of fingers danced together between them, touching and feeling. Occasionally the one would kiss the other's fingertips and they would be back to dancing again. The bed was much less kempt now. Their hearts were less than still, racing with love for the other. When eyes met, they would smile. It was quiet, but the exchange of love continued.

"What are you thinking about?" he asked her.

"You," she said.

He smiled.

"What are you thinking of?"

"You," he replied. "How there's this woman lying next to me who showed grace to me in a way I never could have imagined. I'm so completely unworthy of her, yet here she is by her own will and her own sacrifice, giving herself to me. She could have left me alone in my despair, the way I left her alone in hers, but she didn't. Instead, she presents me with gifts and undeserving praises. Hers is a heart so fragile and so tampered with, and yet she would give it to me to care for. And so I shall, for the rest of my life, handle this oh-so-precious treasure, with appreciation for its pricelessness, as I could never possibly measure its worth."

She smiled. "You must be a writer."

They laughed together and he kissed her fingers again.

"What were you saying to me before?" he said.

"Before we made love?" she asked. "Song of Songs."

"I thought so," he smiled. "Tell me more."

Her smile grew so that her whole body tensed with it. "Place me like a seal over your heart," she said, "like a seal on your arm; for love is as strong as death, its jealousy unyielding as the grave. It burns like blazing fire, like a mighty flame. Many waters cannot quench love; rivers cannot wash it away. If one were to give all the wealth of his house for love, it would be utterly scorned. What's your favorite food?"

Abel squinted at her. "So after Solomon's lover had told him these things, she asked him what his favorite food was?"

Rebecca nodded. "It's right there in scripture." They laughed and she batted at him with her pillow. "What's your favorite food?" she asked again, tucking the pillow beneath her again.

"My favorite food?" he asked.

"Please don't say tuna fish and apples."

He laughed. "Hey, what's wrong with my tuna fish and apples?" He poked her and she squirmed to his light tickle. "Okay, my favorite food," he reverted. "Um... I really like turkey."

"Turkey?" she said. "No, it has to be a junk food."

"With gravy?"

"Try again."

"Okay. I don't know. I don't think you can get too much better than ice cream."

"Mm," she hummed. "Good choice. What kind of ice cream?"
"I'm not sure. Can't really go wrong with vanilla."
"Do you like peanut butter?" she asked.
"Yes, I like peanut butter."
"If I went and got some chocolate and vanilla swirl," she said, "and some peanut butter shell to go over that, would you let me feed you?"
"That would be great," he said. "But you might want to put some clothes on first."
She laughed. "We have it all already." She leaned forward and kissed his nose. Before she could escape from him, he reached out and encircled his hand behind her neck. She beamed her contentment and fell into him, kissing. As she managed to break away, she said, "I'll be right back." He watched her as she grabbed her robe and walked out of the room.

Abel lay back in bed staring at the ceiling high above. He stretched his hands out in front of him. On his left ring finger was the gold band—his wedding ring. He had been wearing it the past few months, even before he and his wife exchanged their vows for a second time, but he hadn't paid much attention to it until now. He spun it on his finger and smiled.

As he tucked his hands behind his head, laying back into his pillow with a contented sigh, he heard a thump come from down the hall, followed by a crash. The sound made him jolt up. He waited for a moment and heard nothing. "Honey?" he said in the direction of the door. No response. He sat on the edge of the bed. "Rebecca?" he called. Still nothing.

He went to the closet and grabbed a pair of jeans, then grabbed a jumbled t-shirt from off the floor putting it on. When he walked through the door, he called for her again: "Rebecca, are you alright?" He walked the length of the hallway, running his hand on the trimming next to him as the house was still quite dark. "Rebecca, can you answer me please?"

He looked around a corner and as soon as he did he felt something strike him on the back of the head. The blow was hard enough that he

lost his balance and fell to the floor. Managing to keep his composure, he shook his head. He wouldn't get up before he was struck again.
"Be a good boy and die."
That was all he heard before he lost consciousness.

Trask had fallen asleep at his desk at the firm. It wasn't the first time. The light of the day was gone. All that was left was the small desk lamp illuminating the paperwork he had been reading over. He sat up in his chair when the phone rang. He tried to wake himself rubbing his eyes. It would take a second ring before he realized what woke him.
"Hello, this is Trask… Yes… You found a note from my wife? What did it say? Uh huh… Yes, call the police. I'll be there as quickly as I can."

Chapter 11

Abel felt himself falling backward. His body seemed twisted and upside down, spinning in the air. He felt like he was back in the car again. He felt like he was back in the driver's seat, hanging upside down. It was his head playing tricks on him. He wasn't going anywhere. He had been propped up in a chair with his hands tied behind his back. His head bobbed, chin thumping against his chest. Drool oozed down onto his shirt. He groaned, trying to lift up his aching head. Managing to throw his head back on his neck, it only fell to bob again.

"You're waking up," came the voice. It was a voice he recognized. Abel was sure of it. But his head was spinning so much, he couldn't discern much of anything.

"Sorry about the headache," the voice said. "You'll feel better in a moment."

Abel attempted to lift his head again. What little light he could distinguish seemed to flicker. It was orange. He could see shadows—figures moving. Everything was still so blurry.

"That's it," came the voice again.

He blinked hard. He tried to focus. Steadily everything came into view.

"Good morning, my love."

Trask had to stop on his way home for the ambulance to pass by him. He followed the emergency vehicle all the way to the house, greeted by medical personnel when he stepped out of his car. "Do you live here?" they asked him.

"Yes, this is my house."

"Did you call?"

"No, my housekeeper did." Trask went rushing through the front door. "Maria?" he called. "Maria?"

She came walking around the corner. "Mr. Trask," she said.

"Maria, did you find her?"

"Mr. Trask. This way." The medicals and the lawyer followed the housekeeper into the hallway. The bathroom door was open with the light on. Trask came to the doorway and saw his wife lying on the floor, hair everywhere, resting facedown in shallow smears of her own blood. He screamed for her, but the medical workers pushed Trask out of the way, coming quickly to her aid. All the while her husband stood by, calling her name.

"It's easier for you to listen when you're awake," the voice came to Abel.

He still couldn't see him, but he knew who it was.

"Greg," he muttered.

"Well, that's the name you knew me by, anyway," the voice said. "That's what I told you to call me when I first came into your house. But it wasn't my first name."

"Tom?" he asked.

"Tom it is," the voice confirmed. "Although you never were too wise to the last name."

"Gregory?"

"Nope," the voice said. "I told you to be careful who you talk to. Didn't I tell you that? I warned you from the very beginning: 'Be careful who you talk to.' You could have been wise to me a long time ago."

"Tom," Abel said, still struggling to speak in his delirious state; "I'm sorry that I fired you."

Tom, formerly known as Greg, who had once claimed to be Abel's manager, burst out laughing. "What? Are you freaking kidding me?

You think I'm doing this because you fired me? Oh, give me a break! You are one high-and-mighty coin pusher, you know that?"

"Why are you doing this?"

"Because you did this to me!" Tom shouted. "I'm taking from you just like you took from me."

"I don't know what you're talking about."

"Oh, come on. Do try."

Abel snarled. "I don't exactly have much of my memory, remember, Greg?"

"Testy, testy," Tom said, clicking his tongue against his teeth. "Besides, you don't have to think back too far before the accident. Who were you driving with?"

"Frank Meadows," Abel said. "Darrel Druse."

"How disappointing. Is David Solis so pathetic that you always have to mention him last?"

"Solis?"

"That's my name," Tom said. "Tom Solis. And you didn't have a clue. My parents may not have cared much for the death of my brother, but I sure did. I can't possibly imagine why they didn't just chuck that trifle money care-package you sent them and tried to sue you for more—didn't try to bleed you dry. I don't know why they didn't just drag you back into court and demand your justly deserved life-sentence. They certainly had the money to best your small-time lawyer any day."

"Your brother," Abel uttered.

"Yes," Tom said. "The one you don't remember. The one who thought you were the greatest thing since great things. The one who emulated you and everything you did. The one who wrote you songs you didn't use."

"He was just a guy at a party," Abel said. "He was just tagging along. Frank told me he was just in the wrong place at the wrong time."

"That's right, Frank," Tom said. "At least he's paralyzed for life. I thought he was going to be a turnip. It never dawned on me that he might possibly snap out of that coma of his. I figured he might try to reveal me so I decided to take it upon myself to get rid of you right away."

"That was you driving the limo?"

Tom laughed. "Hell, no. You think I'm suicidal enough to jump out of a moving vehicle? Come on—I'm crazy, but I'm not that crazy. No, I hired a hit-man to do that."

"A hit-man?"

"Sure. They're not make-believe. Pay one of them enough and they'll do anything for you." Tom poked Abel in the chest with something hard. It was also very hot.

"Ouch," Abel muttered. "You knew my wife's favorite flower. You told me it was the tulip."

"I can get that information from anywhere," Tom said.

"Why?"

"Why tell you her favorite flower?" Tom asked. "Because I wanted you to wine her. I wanted you to dine her. I wanted the two of you to fall desperately in love again. It was all part of the plan—right from the very beginning."

"Tom, where is my wife?"

"Why don't you open your eyes and look?" Tom asked.

Abel raised his head. Rebecca sat not too far across from him next to the fireplace. She was conscious and crying, duct tape covering her mouth and wrapped all the way around her head. She was bonded to her chair more than Abel was to his. He felt his hands wrapped behind his back, behind the chair, and his ankles were taped together as well.

"Greg," Abel said, the adrenaline helping him overcome his wooziness, his heart pounding with what this assailant might try to do. "Greg, Tom, whatever it is you want, I'll get it for you. Do you want more money? Do you want me to take a listen to your brother's songs? Anything. Just name it."

"You know," Tom said, "I love on the radio how they always do those dumb criminal stories? You know those? The thing about committing a crime, like," he snickered, "I've already done here, is that you're instantly guilty. These crooks, the things that make them hit these dumb criminal stories is that they get greedy. That's the one fatal mistake they make every time. They get greedy and do stupid things and get caught. Now, let's just say I took you up on this money-making idea of yours and I say, 'Sure, Abel. Give me summore bucks and I'll leave you and your pretty wife alone.' Do we all live happily ever after? No. I get locked up in jail, don't I?"

He laughed and walked over to the fireplace, sticking in the fire-poker he had been gesturing with. Abel looked down and saw the black burn stain on his shirt where he had been poked—where his skin still tingled from the contact.

"I'm not here for money, Abel," Tom said. "I'm just here to give you what you deserve." Sparks flew from the fire as he poked at the logs. "Revenge," he uttered. "I want you to know what it's like to lose someone you love."

"No, Tom, don't. I beg of you!" Abel's voice shook. He rocked back and forth in his chair. The legs bounced on the floor. The effort made his head spin. He felt sick. "Tom, please," he whimpered. "Do whatever you want to me. Just please don't hurt her."

"Man, I sure wish you could see yourself," Tom said, still poking at the fire. "I wish that you could actually get up out of your chair and observe this scene we're in. I wish you could look and picture the three occupants in your vehicle all sitting around here and say to them, 'Alright everyone, now that we're all liquored up, we're going to go for a drive. Doesn't that sound fun?'" He changed voices and squealed, "Yay! A drive!" Then reverted back; "'That's right, a drive. The catch is: only half of us are going to come out of this alive and the remainder of us will be scarred for life. Now who's with me?'"

Tom continued to prod at the fire, rolling his iron around in the flames. Abel looked at his wife. Tears were dripping off her chin. Her shoulders heaved with her heavy sobs. Her eyes had been locked onto her husband all the while.

"See, what's happening here," Tom continued to monologue, "is that we're going to go for a little ride. One of us is going to come out of this dead. The other two will be scarred for the rest of their lives." The corners of Tom's mouth turned down. His eyes sparkled against the fire light. "I'm already scarred for the rest of my life," he said, choking back tears. "My brother is gone, and nothing is going to bring him back. My brother is gone because you couldn't be just a little responsible. Just a little. Your life was nothing but a great big party. My brother just happened to be in the way."

"Tom," Abel said, "this isn't going to bring David back either. Hurting us is just going to make it hurt worse. It's not going to cure this pain that you feel. Trust me. I know."

"Oh yes," Tom said, starting to laugh again, wiping away with the back of his hand what tears had begun to form. "This is your little sanctimonious stint, right? This is your cure-all asking everyone for forgiveness thing you've been on ever since the accident, isn't it? Hey, whatever helps you sleep at night. I'm sure after all this is over it's going to take a lot more than God to help you sleep at night."

He pulled the poker from the fire and blew on it.

"Preview of coming attractions," he said, holding the poker over Rebecca's face. Her whimpers became quite evident behind her mask of duct tape. She looked at the hot poker, sweat beading and running down her face. "I'm going to take this firing rod," Tom said, "and I'm going to use it first on you." He pointed it right at Abel. "I want you to know exactly what it is little Rebecca here is going to be feeling all the way through this thing."

Tom walked over with the fire poker and picked up a throw-pillow off of the floor. He placed the pillow firmly over Abel's face and thrust the hot poker into Abel's side. Abel's body jerked. His legs straightened and shook. His toes fanned out. Beneath the pillow came his muffled cries. He wailed in pain and the red hot piece of metal pressed against his flesh. The heat from the poker burned the t-shirt away from his skin. Abel twisted his body, trying to squirm away from the touch of the poker, but it was no use. The torture was no more than ten seconds, but the burn would be felt even after Tom pulled the poker away from his body and the pillow off of his face.

Abel couldn't breathe. He gasped and panted, his face saturated with a mixture of sweat and spit from having the pillow covering him. He twisted his body to the side he was gouged. It hurt so much. Even after it was over, the pain was still there.

"Wonderful feeling, isn't it?" Tom asked. "Cool thing about it is the wound cauterizes itself from the heat. Even if I do happen to stab you too deeply, I don't have to worry about you bleeding to death. However, there is always that possibility of dying from shock. In which case, God can only be so merciful to let it happen."

Abel coughed and cried, the moisture on his face being mixed with his tears. "You freak," he muttered. "You sick freak."

Tom only chuckled, sticking the poker back in the fire, ready to heat it up for the next victim. Abel's head drooped over his lap, huffing and panting, wincing from the pain. He lifted his eyes and looked at his wife, sobbing behind the tape on her mouth. He wouldn't let that psychopath do that to her. He couldn't. But what could he do?

Abel planted his feet firmly on the floor, looking menacingly toward the torturous executioner cooking his instrument in the fire. Before he could think, before any other thought came into his mind, he pushed as hard as he could and flung into the air, yelling.

The action caught the attention of Tom, but there was nothing he could do about Abel—feet bound, hands behind him, using his body and the chair to tackle Tom into the fireplace. As soon as Abel made contact with him, he fell straight down to the floor. The same couldn't be said for Tom, falling into the fire, engulfed in flames. Screams came from within as Tom scrambled to get himself out.

The poker fell on the floor.

Abel discovered he was not actually attached to the chair. He could slip his hands over the top and then squirmed his way over to the poker. Rolling himself over on his back, he tried to get the poker into his hands, and let the hot tip rest on the duct tape. He winced, gnashing his teeth in pain from the heat, ultimately melting through the tape and breaking his hands free.

The blazing Tom managed to scurry onto the living room rug and rolled around, beating on his body, attempting to extinguish the flames eating through his clothing, screaming and groaning all the more as the heat bit into his flesh.

Abel pushed the tape off of his ankles, wriggling his feet out of it, running over to his wife and attempting to pull her free from her trappings. He wasn't paying attention to Tom, feeling like the fire was enough to keep his adversary occupied. However, Tom was just getting to his feet.

Abel pulled the tape off of Rebecca's mouth, painfully, but she let her scream of agony form the words, "Behind you!"

Abel spun around just in time to catch the poker before it could skewer either he or his wife, Tom holding on to the other end of it, sinews sparkling on his shoulders from the fire he'd extinguished, smoke rising and encircling his head. He punched Tom across the jaw, throwing him off balance enough to release his grip on the poker. With a baseball swing, Abel socked Tom in the lower abdomen with the hot poker. Tom coughed and gagged feeling the air get knocked out of him.

The next swing and Tom managed to grab the poker, burning his hands but it was better than the strike he would have received. He pulled the weapon out of Abel's hands, growling, but Abel didn't let him get the upper hand. He threw his body into him, propelling the both of them backwards. The small of Tom's back connected with the open piano behind him. Abel picked him up and threw him, slamming the lid down on top of him.

Tom shouted his displeasure and tried pushing his way out. The piano wasn't deep enough to keep him inside. As he tried to climb out, Abel punched him again, knocking him back into the strings. With all his might, Abel got his hands up under the grand piano and heaved as hard as he could, tipping it over on its side so that the lid mashed up against the wall, trapping the occupant inside. The piano landed with a dissonant song.

The burning embers on Tom's clothing had singed Abel's shirt which he promptly tore off and threw to the floor. Abel went straight back to his wife, kissing her face before trying to remove the tape that bound her. "I'm fine," she said to him. "Call the police first."

Tom continued to bang from inside the piano, shouting. The vibration from the noise he created echoed through the strings of the instrument making haunting, harrowing sounds.

"Yes, this is Abel West," he said into the phone. "We've had a break-in. Someone tried to kill us—my wife and me. Please send someone… Yes, he's still in the house. We have him trapped." Abel gave them the address and ran back to Rebecca. "Let's get you out of here."

By the time the couple hobbled out of the house, blankets wrapped around them, the first of the emergency dispatch was just arriving. Two police cars pulled up, lights blaring in blues and reds, shining spots upon Abel and Rebecca as they got out with guns drawn.

"It's okay," Abel shouted at them. "We're alright."

"Where's the burglar?" one of the officers shouted.

"He's inside," Abel said. "He's… in the piano."

Two of the officers looked at each other, seemingly perplexed, before darting inside.

More sirens sounded in the distance. Abel and Rebecca were helped to an ambulance. When the blanket fell from around them, Abel's wounds were exposed and he winced in pain. The emergency workers separated them to different vehicles. Rebecca cried for him in disapproval.

"It's okay," Abel said to her. "Let them take you. It'll be alright."

She reached out for him with outstretched fingers. "Please don't leave me!"

"I'm right here," Abel called back to her. "I won't leave you." They laid him back on a stretcher as he continued to mumble, "I won't leave you."

"We're right here," a nurse said over him. "You've breathed in some smoke. We just want to be safe." She placed an oxygen mask over his face.

"Jesus…" Abel whispered.

"That's some pretty nasty burns you have there," the nurse said.

"Thank you, Jesus."

Outside the ambulance, the rain began to fall. Over all the sounds, the commotion, the rain brought a soothing calm. Quieting. Still.

Trask pinched the bridge of his nose, eyes closed, resting quietly in the chair he'd been sitting in for the past several hours. A nurse had previously brought him something for his headache. Two empty cups rest on the small table next to him along with a Gideon's Bible.

There wasn't much his mind would settle on. His thoughts couldn't quite assemble the words together in the note his wife had left him, found by his housemaid—the poor woman. "Tell Alexander," it began. She wouldn't even address him personally. She distanced herself from him so. The letter would go on to say that her being alive had no reason anymore. She only destroyed the lives she was introduced to. There was no sense in continuing to subject people to having to tolerate her. Something along those lines.

The blood that transferred from her body to his clothes when he had clung to her in the ambulance blended in with the combinations of darks that he wore, looking as though he had only gotten wet. After a while of being unable to get anyone to speak to him about his wife's condition, he released his worry in prayer and had been sitting here ever since.

"Mr. Trask?"

He snapped right to at being addressed, rising to greet the doctor that was speaking to him. "Yes, that's me," he said, the doctor standing in the doorway of the waiting room.

"Your wife is fine," the doctor said firstly. Trask bowed his head and breathed a silent prayer of thanks. "Fortunately the cuts on her wrists were not deep enough to cause any fatal blood loss. We did have to give her blood and she's resting comfortably."

"Is she awake?" he asked.

"She's resting comfortably," the doctor said again.

"What room is she in? Can I see her?"

"Your wife didn't want to be disturbed. She specifically ask that she didn't receive any…"

Trask grabbed the clipboard from the doctor and looked at it.

"Now, sir," the doctor protested, reaching for the clipboard, trying to pull it from him as Trask skimmed the notes. He released the clipboard and started down the hall.

"Sir, you can't just go down there!" the doctor called after him. "Sir, visiting hours are over!" The doctor tried to catch up to him. "The cuts in her face were awfully deep. We had to wait for the swelling to go down before we could stitch the cuts together. There is some permanent scarring, but with some plastic surgery she may be able to reconstruct…"

"Someone tell me where I'm going here!" Trask shouted, as he read the numbers at the top of the doorways. "Where's number…" He saw where the numbers continued down an adjoining hallway.

"Sir, it would be best if you just come back another time."

He came to the door and stood in front of it.

Just as he was about to enter, the doctor caught up to him and grabbed his arm. "Come on, sir. She said she didn't want…"

Trask jerked his arm angrily away from the doctor and loudly sounded, "Shh!" holding his hand up. He placed his hand on the handle, closing his eyes, just breathing, pushing down on the handle and stepping into the dark room.

The door closed behind him in its two-sound click. He stood now in the indigo melancholy. The room was crying. Patterns created from the rain streaking down the window panes, letting in the only little bit of light, crawled down the walls and across half of the floor. All corners were blackened creating a rounded effect to the room. He identified where she sat, there at the edge of her bed with her back to him. He looked at her for a moment with disappointment, but didn't want her to see a face like this. He looked at his hands by his sides as the rain trickled down disappearing at the ends of his fingers.

He walked toward her carefully.

She could hear his footsteps and spoke when he started to move: "I didn't want to see anybody."

He stopped moving and stood there, reconsidering his approach.

"I know," he said softly, a deep baritone voice absorbed into the shadows.

"Why are you here?" she said, followed by a sniffle.

He sighed, taking another step forward ending up at the corner of the bed that was furthest away from her. His middle finger lightly brushed against the top spread. "Why don't you want me to be?"

Her back straightened some, then sagged again as she let out another sob. "I just don't want to hurt you anymore."

He would look at her every time she said something, then find his eyes back down at his hands. "This hurts me."

"Then why don't you leave me?" she said, letting her head drop with the rest of her body.

"Because I love you."

"But why?" On the question, her head turned a little toward him. But just as soon as she did this, she turned even more away, even twisting her body to show him more of her back.

He took the two steps more he needed to be at the next corner of the foot of the bed. "I don't think I need a reason." When he spoke, revealing his position, his wife turned her head completely to the wall so not to show him her face. "Why do you hide from me?" he asked her.

"Because I'm no good to you," she said with a whimper. "I never have been."

"Don't you think I should be the judge of that?" he asked. He stepped out in front of the bed, standing there for a moment, perhaps waiting to see if she'd retreat from him further. With one more foot forward, he sat down on the edge of the bed next to her.

"Just let me go," she whispered, barely audible.

"I'm not going to do that," he replied.

"I'm so messed up," she whispered again.

"I haven't been doing the best job I could have either," he said.

"Alex, I betrayed you. What could you have done that could possibly have been worse than that?"

"I could only assume you went to another man for love because of something I did," he said. "Or didn't do. I've been married to my work. Then I committed myself to Abel and his case. I haven't made time for you."

"No, it was nothing like that," she said. "You've always been so good to me. I'm just so messed up." She put her face in her hands and began to cry.

"Don't do that," he said. "You'll mess up your stitches." He pulled lightly at her wrist with his fingertips, but she rolled her hand away from him. When he tried for it again, she relented, letting it float down to the bed-top where he held the back of her hand in his palm.

The uneven hair she had left on that side of her head covered over her face, a fabric shadow between his eyes and hers. He reached out to brush it back, pushing away the curtain she hid behind, but she turned her head away with a soft, "No."

"Just let me look at you," he said.

She shook her head, sobbing.

"Why are you like this?"

"Because I don't know any other way to be," she said.

"Then just let me love you," he said.

"Why can't you just hate me?"

"What makes me want to hate you?"

She turned her face to him. "Because I look like this!"

She was veiled in shadow, but he could see the change in definition. She ran scissors in X-marks up and down her face. One side of her mouth was so badly cut that it wouldn't stay closed anymore. On the other side, an eye grazed over and swelled shut. They were all deep enough to be permanent scars, sewn together and mended by multiple stitches like a reassembled rag-doll. Her face would always be beyond recognition of the appearance she was before.

He tried not to show indifference to what she had done to herself, trying to keep his courtroom face, but the tears that brimmed on the edge of his eyes said otherwise.

"Why did you do this to yourself," he asked.

"I just didn't feel beautiful anymore," she sobbed. Her eyes, though one tightly clasped, still managed to produce her tears. "I felt disgusted with myself. I just couldn't stand to look at myself or live with myself anymore."

"Because you can't let go," he said. "I forgave you a long time ago. This has happened to you because you can't let it go. You still blame yourself. You still hide behind a garbage mound of guilt. I can't live like that, and neither can you." He stopped and looked toward the window at the rain, half of him sitting in shadow and the other half dripping in waterfalls. "But…"

He turned his head back and looked down at the hand he was holding. Steadily, he inched more toward her on the bed, trailing out of the bit of light that was there and joined her in her shadow. "I don't have enough to care for us both," he said. "I'm not strong enough. No one is. I have love to give you. I've been trying to give that to you for a long time now. But if you want these things, you have to accept them. It's not just enough that I love you or forgive you. You have to want that for yourself. They're yours to have. I'm not going to give them to anyone else."

"I don't know how to receive them," she said.

"Let me show you the way," he said.

He rest his forehead against hers and could feel her tremble. He could feel her shakes all the way through the bed.

"How could you ever want this face again," she murmured.

He pulled his head away and looked at her. He couldn't feel her trembling as much, but that could have been because he was shaking too. He lifted both hands to her face, caressing where the skin was smooth on her neck, unblemished and untouched. There at his fingertips he could feel her heart race. He felt her heart beat for him.

He leaned forward and twisted his mouth in such a way that his lips would fit together with hers. She reached up and clutched his wrists in her hands, trembling. She swallowed when their lips touched, so unsteady, so incredibly fragile in his care. Her hands fell the length of his arms, reaching up behind his head and running her fingers into his hair.

The kiss was long, but gentle. Both of them were crying before it was over.

"Thank you," she whispered.

He shook his head slightly, resting his forehead against hers. "It's over now."

Chapter 12

The interlaced fingers joining the hands of Abel and Rebecca rest between them in their seats as they sat listening intently to the pastor's message. They sat on the end of the aisle with Jared, Emily, and their family. To the outside was a new member of their church-going group. There was a woman that they had only recently met. She came to accompany her husband, Frank Meadows, who was sitting on his own in his own chair at the end of the row, no longer requiring the use of a wheelchair to get around. They all sat listening to the sermon composed by the pastor that had led the services in Abel and Rebecca's remarriage.

The highlights of his message were being shown in bright graphics on the overhead behind him. The scripture reference was from Luke 17.

"How many times are we supposed to forgive? When do we run out? How much forgiveness are we meant to forgive before we are told we don't have to forgive anymore? Are we supposed to forgive seven times? Seven times and that's it? You get seven chances and that's all you get? In Luke chapter seventeen verse four, Jesus said, 'If someone wrongs you seven times in a day, and seven times comes back to you and says, 'I repent,' forgive him.' Seven times in a day? Is that all we get?"

The scripture reference on the overhead changed to Matthew 18.

"How about seventy times?" the pastor suggested. "Seventy times in a day: well that's something I can handle. I think I can make few enough mistakes that I can be forgiven and still have a few left to spare if it's seventy times. In Matthew, Peter comes to Jesus and says,

'Lord, how many times should I forgive? Up to seven times?' Jesus, said to Peter, 'No, I tell you not just seven times, but seventy times seven.' What is that, four-hundred and ninety times? Is that right?" He got confirmation from someone in the congregation. "Thank you. My mental math isn't all that great." The congregation chuckled.

"What is Jesus saying here?" the pastor asked. "Is Jesus saying that we can be forgiven only four-hundred and ninety times and that's it? No. Jesus wasn't preaching a specific number here. Jesus was telling us to keep on forgiving until we're blue in the face. Just keep on dishing it out, man. There's more of this forgiveness to go around. Now, I understand that when someone wrongs you, there's a trust violated in that. Jesus acknowledged that too. The first part of that verse we read in Luke chapter seventeen verse three says if someone wrongs you, rebuke him. There's nothing wrong with that. But then it says if he repents, forgive him. So we are commanded to do."

The pastor set his Bible down on the pulpit and stepped out to address the congregation beyond his notes.

"There are plenty of places in this world to exercise forgiveness," the pastor said. "If you're not exercising it, you're just wasting a good muscle that God has given to you to use and to build up. Exercising forgiveness is good for the soul, folks. It's good for your heart; not only spiritually, but I'm sure if you talked to any psychologist, they would tell you it's good for you physically as well." The pastor absentmindedly had gestured in Dr. Ellis Corin's direction. Dr. Corin smiled and nodded.

"Who do we have to forgive? Who needs forgiveness? Forgiveness is not only for the person you are extending grace to, it's for you as well. Without it, you bottle all this stuff up, and that can create a whole lot of ugly. You don't need any of that. Maybe you have to forgive your spouse. It may be the tiniest of mistakes, like impatiently trying to rush them out the door this morning on your way to church. But you lost your patience, and you need to apologize to them for that. That's okay. Spouse, if your significant other apologizes to you, you need to forgive them."

Rebecca elbowed Abel at the suggestion. Abel scowled at her playfully. She smiled.

"Maybe you need to forgive your mom or dad. Maybe they did something a long time ago to you that you've been harboring inside of you for years. Let it go. Forgive them. Maybe you need to forgive someone who's dead and gone. Can you still forgive those people? Yes, you can. And you should. Let it go. Not every time that we ask for forgiveness are we going to be met with the answer that we want if we even get an answer at all. Forgiveness doesn't have to be issued by any person to be received, and to receive it when no one has given it, you need to learn to forgive yourself. Forgiveness is all around us. It's floating around us like air. All you need to do is take it. Confess yourself before God. God says he'll give it to you. And he will remember your wrongdoings no more. God with amnesia. Isn't it cool? Someone give me an amen!"

The congregation said, "Amen" in unison.

The pastor added, "Won't you accept a little bit of Jesus into your lives today?"

"Speech! Speech! Speech! Speech! Speech!"

The gathering at the celebration begged for their guest of honor to grace them with words of appreciation and acceptance. Pushed up in front of them all, the gentleman in black stood before a waiting crowd putting his hands up, one occupied by a champagne glass, and waited for them to quiet.

Behind him was a banner that boldly displayed his latest project. Next to it was another banner—an expanded-sized version of a page taken from the magazine charts boldly proclaiming Benjamin Paul's newest album at the number one slot in sales for the week.

When he had his audience's attention, Benjamin Paul spoke from the table-top on which he stood. "Thank you so very much everyone for coming tonight. This entertainment corporation we've established here has been a dream of mine as well as the shared dream of some other individuals. I hope you know that when an album like this one here," he gestured to the banner behind him, "does so well in such a secular market that the accomplishment is not mine alone but the contribution of several individuals to this cause. Even though I did all the work myself."

Several people laughed and booed at once, all in good fun.

Benjamin pointed at someone specifically and laughed. "No, I'm just kidding. I'm grateful to you all. This is the first project where I've willingly opened myself up to other writers. It's also the first project to debut at number one. I'm sure that's reflective enough of what can be accomplished through collaborative effort, and I thank you all."

The crowd of a hundred or so people applauded and cheered.

Benjamin Paul held up his hand again to dismiss the acclaim. "Speaking of songwriters," he said, waiting for them to quiet again. "Speaking of songwriters, this new album also marked bringing in someone new to our family here—a couple of new persons, actually. Cowering over there by the refreshment table..." He gestured toward the back of the room and everyone turned around and looked with a murmur of chuckling. "The couple standing back there with one another is Abel West—which I'm sure is a name a lot of you recognize—and his wife Rebecca. Abel has joined our catalogue. We now own every song written by Abel West and every song he will ever write for the rest of his life."

The audience laughed and applauded.

"Are you feeling that ball and chain yet?" Benjamin called out to him.

Abel laughed, embarrassed.

"His wife, Rebecca," Benjamin continued, "has joined our publishing group. She has a passion for this organization as much as the rest of us and she's going to help take Benjamin Press to the next level. We're opening up a whole new department of not just music publishing but books, magazines, anthologies, text books, and whatever else we think we can positively contribute to our culture and the world through this organization. We've been blessed enough to be expanding, and so I just want to thank the West's for wanting to be a part of all of this that we're doing here. I know you'll warmly welcome them into this commission we've set forth to achieve. God bless you all."

Everyone applauded as Benjamin Paul hopped off of the table and rejoined the party. The music started back up. The patrons visited with one another over their normal speaking voices. The activity went on most of the night—complete with dining, dancing, conversation, and more.

Rebecca was dancing with Frank, hobbling on a cane, legs stiff with the braces that held him up, talking and laughing with him. Abel mouthed words to her and was quite tickled with the both of them as he and Benjamin continued to visit with one another outside of the dance floor.

"I can't think you enough for all of this, Ben."

"It's my pleasure," Benjamin said. "Really, take credit for this album going to number one. You were just as much a part of it as anyone else."

"The way I understand it, you extend yourself a lot for other people," Abel said. "Why would you do that? Especially since most of these people have never given you anything in the first place. Why put yourself out there like that?"

"When you write songs," Benjamin said, "aren't you putting your heart out there every day in the songs that you are writing for people you don't even know?"

"Yeah," Abel said, "I can relate to that."

"It's part of the business," Benjamin said. "Songwriting is very honest. It's very giving—if you're going about it that way. Are you familiar with Proverbs chapter three?"

"'Trust in the Lord with all your heart and lean not on your own understanding'?" Abel asked.

"Good one," Ben said. "But no, after that. Verse twenty-seven I believe."

"You'll have to refresh my memory."

"'Do not withhold good from those who deserve it when it is in your power to act.'"

"Mm," Abel nodded. "Good verse." He thought for a moment. "But I didn't do anything to lead you to believe I deserved any blessing."

"You didn't have to," Benjamin smiled.

Abel chuckled. "And here we are."

"How have the two of you been since that episode at your house?" Benjamin asked.

"Oh, we're fine," Abel said. "I don't think we were too afraid to be home after that. We just couldn't believe that a person could be driven to do things like that."

"It's what all of us would be like without grace," Benjamin said.

"Interesting way of putting that," Abel said. "I guess sometimes I don't consider I'm just as capable of being just as destructive. And I was. But I'm forgiven. It's very purifying. My brother told me that blame is just one person's opinion."

"I'd say your brother is a wise man," Benjamin said.

"I sometimes feel that the guilt will never go away," Abel said. "Not entirely anyway. I mean, I know I'm forgiven, but there's still something there, you know? And especially after the intruder in our home. I still couldn't help but feel somehow responsible."

"That," Benjamin smiled, "is why grace is so amazing, isn't it? There's nothing wrong with feeling guilty. It's sometimes a very necessary human emotion. How could we acknowledge and accept grace if we didn't recognize we needed it first? It's when we let the pain consume our souls that it becomes the problem."

"I've figured that out," Abel said.

"Think you could write a song about that?" Benjamin asked.

Abel smiled. "I already have."

GABRIEL PETER

Lord I've tried to see
All you've done for me
I gave you my burden
But I'm not so sure I'm
Burdenless
I've yet
Been able to forget
The prayer that I prayed you
And all that I claim to
Have confessed
You take these cares of mine
And you throw them all away
But I guess my mind
Doesn't quite work the same way
How far is...

East from west to me
Maybe I try to hard to see
My water turn to wine
Or another burning bush type of sign
How can it be
Your forgiveness lifted me
And of what I do confess
Is thrown as far as east is from the west

Lord I'm trying to
Do what you have me do
But I've been so weighed down
Despite having laid down
All my cares
So hard
To let go of my heart
Can't be too choosing

EAST FROM WEST

In this game of
Musical chairs
You take these cares from me
And remember them no more
But my memory
Is so hard to ignore
How far is...

East from west to me
Maybe I try too hard to see
My water turn to wine
Or another burning bush type of sign
How can it be
Your forgiveness lifted me
And of what I do confess
Is thrown as far as east is from the west

I cannot perceive
These hearts of ours
May be endlessly naïve
But we grow strong
If we just believe.
Just believe.